Literature for Life Series
General Editor : Kenyon Calthrop

Short Stories from Scotland

Selected and introduced by John Blackburn

Frontispiece by Peter Kesteven

Wheaton A Division of Pergamon Press

A. Wheaton & Company Limited, *A Division of Pergamon Press*, Hennock Road, Exeter EX2 8RP

Pergamon Press Ltd, Headington Hill Hall, Oxford OX3 0BW

Pergamon Press Inc., Maxwell House, Fairview Park, Elmsford, New York 10523

Pergamon of Canada Ltd, 75 The East Mall, Toronto, Ontario M8Z 2L9

Pergamon Press (Australia) Pty Ltd, 19a Boundary Street, Rushcutters Bay, N.S.W. 2011

Pergamon Press GmbH, 6242 Kronberg/Taunus, Pferdstrasse 1, Frankfurt-am-Main, Federal Republic of Germany

First edition 1979

Printed in Great Britain by A. Wheaton & Co. Ltd, Exeter (BW)

ISBN 0 08 021885 7

Contents

Acknowledgements

For permission to reprint the stories included in this book, we are indebted to:

Wm Collins & Sons Ltd for *The Deprived* by Janet Caird, and *Spud: Suffering through Sunday* by William Grant, both published in *Collins Scottish Short Stories*.

Iain Crichton Smith for *The Blot, Jimmy and the Policeman* and *The Wedding*.

Curtis Brown Ltd for *Scotch Settlement* by Neil Paterson, originally published in the *Penguin Book of Short Stories*, and *Smeddum* by Lewis Grassic Gibbon, published in *Scots Hairst*.

The Hogarth Press Ltd for *Five Green Waves* by George Mackay Brown, originally published in a *Calendar of Love and Other Stories*.

The School of Scottish Studies, University of Edinburgh, and also Alan Bruford, Robert Garioch and Hamish Henderson, for *The Three Feathers* by Andra Stewart.

Introduction

W HEN I began to put this collection together I thought it likely that it would contain a fair number of stories from times well before our own, for it does not seem reasonable to believe that only modern literature is of relevance to us as "literature for life". As things turned out, the collection has in it only two stories which were written before the present century—for the simple reason that those stories from earlier times which seemed most suitable are already available in other anthologies. Some eyebrows, however, may be raised at the inclusion of *Thrawn Janet* and of *Smeddun* yet again. More eyebrows would, I think, have been raised by their omission, particularly since the only currently available anthology in which they both appear is J. M. Reid's, in the Oxford Classics series, published in 1963.

In choosing the stories for this collection I have had no theme in mind. Themes, it seems to me, if deliberately sought for or held in view, are altogether too liable to lead one to distort or to devalue the particular blend of experience inherent in a piece of literature. Nor, for that matter, did I seek any particular mood, though in retrospect I am pleased that the general tone is one of affirmation. Despair and loss of direction and the raw and the horrible require sober acknowledgement, but, for the main part, it seems best to be positively and coherently in favour of living.

The language in some of the stories may be found strange by those who live outside the areas of origin. I trust that, overall, no undue difficulty will be experienced. Six of the eleven stories are in English, or at least some variety of it, and only two of the rest are wholly in some form of Scots. Besides, there is a glossary which will, I hope, prove useful when the need arises.

There are two sorts of story which, though common enough among the works of Scots writers, do not match the spirit of the present series, and accordingly they are scarcely represented. I refer to tales of the macabre and to the anecdotes of the kailyard writers.

Tales of the macabre have for long been part of the Scottish scene. These, however, achieve their effects not by evoking the world with which we are familiar, but rather by introducing into that world things and events which are foreign to it—curious, unpredictable, malevolent. They are not, therefore, particularly appropriate in a series concerned principally with the world as we find it.

The term *kailyard,* among Scottish men of letters, is applied to a sort of writing which flourished near the turn of the century and which came, as it were, from one's own cabbage-patch, one's yard of kail or kale. In it there is no place for wild and disturbing passion or for keen and disturbing thought or, for that matter, for any marked degree of coarseness in language or of physical detail. The "feel" of the kailyard is essentially nice, trivial, sentimental, comfortably secure. As one lady remarked of it, "You know the girls are nice girls because they always come to the door with dabs of flour on their noses." And they are never likely to exclaim more than "Jings" or "Michty me". It is a world which could quite easily accommodate the nursing home of the first story, *The Deprived.* The unreality in the macabre may be accepted for the effects it creates or the sheer entertainment it affords, but in these kailyard pieces one cannot but conclude that the odd view of life presented is the result of cultivated myopia rather than of creative intent.

The kailyard no longer characterises our writing as once it did. Our novelists, the best of them, are now "significant" again; and among poets there is more vital activity than, it seems, there has ever been. But it would be naïve to imagine that the kailyard has altogether gone. Far from it. It sprang to life again as I browsed for this collection, often in stories hot from the press, and it has blossomed for decades on the stage, in television shows and in weekly periodicals. Other countries and other areas have their kailyards too, of course, but ours, most critics seem agreed, has, for reasons too complex to enter into here, been unusually prominent in social, religious and cultural life.

> This is the land God gave to Andy Stewart—we have our
> inheritance.
> There shall be no ardour, there shall be indifference.
> There shall not be excellence, there shall be the average.
> We shall be the intrepid hunters of golf balls.*

Like most satire, this is not altogether fair—but it is certainly apt.

So, no kailyard and not much macabre. What then of our collection and of our authors?

Janet Caird (b. 1913) is an experienced writer of fiction. She has several novels and one children's book to her credit. *The Deprived,* a recent story, provides in its setting and in its firm, precise tone a contrast to some of the more roughly textured stories which follow it.

*From "The White Air of March" by Iain Crichton Smith.

Neil Paterson's (b. 1916) first novel, *The China Run*, appeared in 1948. Since then he has written a number of novels which have reached a wide public. *Scotch Settlement* was the source of a film, *The Kidnappers*. Though the setting of the story is far from Scotland, its characters can be in no way unfamiliar to any who are acquainted with regions where small farming and the stern ideals of a puritan belief hold sway.

William Grant's *Spud: Suffering through Sunday*, like a good deal of the fiction being written in Scotland today, is about people in the industrial working class. Writers like Grant often seem less concerned with shaping fiction than with providing an expression of "voices of our kind". The blend of humour and wretchedness, of friendly familiarity and lurking violence, which one associates with the great grey stretches of the industrial west, is well caught by this kind of writing.

Lewis Grassic Gibbon (1901–35) is best known for his novel *Sunset Song*, the first in the trilogy *A Scots Quair*. The *Quair* was published in 1969, but the novels themselves were written between 1932 and 1937. Gibbon was also a writer of short stories, and of these *Smeddum* is probably the most well known. It is written in the vigorous and unorthodox manner that is characteristic of Gibbon's best work.

Rab and His Friends is one of the many pieces, mainly essays and letters, written by Dr John Brown (1810–82), who spent most of his life as a general practitioner in Edinburgh. In Brown's writings one finds at times something of that sort of sentiment and moral tone which, in excess, are features of the kailyard. But Brown was too restrained as a writer, and as a man too respectful of fact and of learning, to let sentiment run to excess, and *Rab* is a well-wrought and strangely authentic tale. To Sir J. A. Hammerton, writing in the early thirties, it was "one of the undying things of our literature."

The same might well be claimed for *Thrawn Janet*, a story which has more to it than its macabre effect, as anyone with a healthy suspicion of book learning and of complacent rationalism will quickly perceive. Robert Louis Stevenson (1850–94) was a master craftsman and has many notable works to his credit. Some of these, like *The Master of Ballantrae* and *Weir of Hermiston*, are better known inside Scotland than elsewhere, but others, such as *Kidnapped, The Strange Case of Dr Jekyll and Mr Hyde, Treasure Island* and the autobiographical *Travels with a Donkey in the Cevennes*, have long been regarded as classics of their kind. One of the remarkable things about Stevenson was the number of genres he could handle with success—and that in the course of a relatively short life. Even within his short stories one finds a surprising range of subjects and effects.

For the tale of *The Three Feathers* we are indebted to the School of Scottish Studies, University of Edinburgh. It is a version of *Silly Jack the Water Carrier*, another telling of which is to be found among *Grimms' Fairy Tales*. Literature for life? Certainly. The performance of the hero and of the story-teller, Andra Stewart of Blairgowrie, guarantee that.

Iain Crichton Smith (b. 1928), represented here by *The Wedding* and by two stories from his recently published book *The Village,* has been recognised since the late 1950s as being one of the most accomplished of our poets writing in English. (He writes also in his native Gaelic.) In recent years his output of prose work has increased. Inherent in Crichton Smith's writing is his concern to define and to examine the conditions of that mode of being we call grace. Clearly there can be no adequate discussion of the state of grace in introductory notes like these. Suffice it to remark that it may be seen as involving a feeling of inner harmony and a willingness to extend well-wishing, blessing, to those around one. It is an experience "partly aesthetic, partly theological". From his writing it appears that there are two principal pre-conditions for grace. One is the ability to face truth, as well as one can conceive of it, steadily, without flinching or hiding in illusions or self-deception. And the other is the ability to escape from isolation and to find oneself in relation to one's neighbours, one's community. Both of these conditions are encapsulated in the stories chosen for this collection.

George Mackay Brown (b. 1916), of Orkney, is one of the best-known contemporary Scottish writers. He has written many works of prose and of poetry. His work is often characterised by an accumulation of vignettes, whereby event is added to event, character follows character. Such structuring is expressive of his cyclic, ritualistic conception of the nature of life and of death. The seasons return and life passes through its phases, and we mark these with symbol and ritual. In Mackay Brown's work too there is a close involvement with the physical and the elemental. *Five Green Waves* seems to me to be one of the best of his many highly distinctive pieces of writing.

I hope the stories gathered here will make for some enjoyable reading, and that they will at the same time give some idea of the range of writing in Scotland in recent years.

John Blackburn

The Deprived

Janet Caird

I REMEMBER the very first time I saw The Roses thinking what a wonderful exercise in camouflage it was. On that beautiful June day with the sun blazing, and the famous rose-beds in their first outburst of bloom, it looked wonderful.

The long low house with its old grey sandstone walls covered with Gloire de Dijon roses was charming, and the extensions had been skilfully added at the back so as not to spoil the effect when one emerged from the shady drive into the open ground before the house. The entrance hall prolonged the effect; low-ceilinged, with a wide shallow beautiful wooden staircase leading from it. Everywhere gleaming wood, beautiful rugs, and a huge silver rose-bowl filled with flowers reflected in an antique mahogany table. If it wasn't a fine old country house, it must be a very good hotel: and even though one knew it wasn't, it was a shock when the crisp white uniform of a nurse appeared to ask your business. I got used to the set-up, of course, but the first impression was always at the back of my mind through all the long months when I visited my Aunt Sophia there.

Aunt Sophia was the last member of my mother's family. With the exception of a brother drowned at sea, they had all lived well into their eighties. My mother had reached eighty-nine. Aunt Sophia was ninety-two. She, alone of the family, was extremely wealthy, having been left what seemed to the rest of the family a vast fortune by a doting husband. She was childless and had been a wonderful aunt to all her nieces and nephews. When at last it became clear that she must have skilled nursing, and it being impossible to find private help, it was only natural that she should move into The Roses: The Roses being, in the geriatric world, the equivalent of Claridge's or the

1

Savoy in the normal world. I don't know what the fees were at The Roses, all that being handled by Sophia's lawyers, but they were certainly vast.

Not that the inmates didn't get value for money. They did. The furnishings, food, nursing were all of the highest standard. Everywhere the emphasis was on immaculate freshness, cleanliness, perfection. The roses in the flower-vases always seemed newly picked. I never saw a fallen petal or a faded flower all the time I visited there. It was the acme of discreet good taste. No effort, no detail, was spared to veil the reality of the slow drifting from life of the patients.

And this was more than an elaborate exercise in public relations. When I came down from Aunt Sophia's room on that first day, I was met by a discreet and charming secretary who asked me to call in at Dr Mactaggart-Thom's office. Dr Mactaggart-Thom was medical director and part-owner of The Roses. I must admit that I went in with some prejudice. He would, I was sure, be large, smooth, smell of expensive aftershave and have soft white hands. Not at all. Dr Mactaggart-Thom was certainly tall but very lean, brown (he was a keen fisherman and commuted to Scotland whenever possible), with a firm grasp and a faint tang of snuff. It was all rather reassuring after the smooth perfection outside his office. Dr Mactaggart-Thom was, among other things, an astute businessman. He was also, and with absolute sincerity, passionately interested in and concerned about his patients.

He greeted me courteously, motioned me to a chair and said, "I always like to have a little chat with our guests' nearest relatives. I understand you are in the position of being Mrs Hope's next-of-kin."

"Yes, I am."

"I like to explain just what the principle is on which we run The Roses, so that friends and relations can play their part in the therapeutic arrangements."

"Therapeutic?" I said. "I should have thought any curative procedures were not on . . . "

"Ah, there you are mistaken, Mrs Grant. Some of our guests *do* go back home. But I agree, for the majority, that is not possible. So our aim must be to keep them happy. You may have noticed that we do our best to make their surroundings here as far removed from a hospital atmosphere as possible. . . . "

I made affirmatory noises.

"But we go further. We never, I repeat never, mention the possibility of—ah—their final departure. Our nurses are instructed never to hint at such a thing, or even discuss it among themselves. And we earnestly ask relatives and friends to do the same."

"You mean," I said, "that we must never use the word – "

He raised a hand. "Please. It is never uttered in here. Except perhaps by a guest who has newly arrived. But they soon stop using it, and indeed, I am convinced, even thinking of it, surrounded as they are by so many of the pleasant things of life. And if they ever do show signs of—ah—restiveness, we calm them down."

"With drugs?"

"Various ways and means. A little hypnotic treatment, a glass of good wine . . . . The thing is, they are kept cheerful, happy, and do not think of the future. . . . We protect them from it."

He paused. I was silent, thinking of my mother's last illness and the year she had spent in the local geriatric hospital, a place supplied with all the necessities and none of the luxuries; a place of humour and sadness and steady indestructible human courage, where, as my mother had remarked casually one day, "the wings are always hovering", and no one had any illusions about the outcome . . .

"You don't approve?" Dr Mactaggart-Thom had a penetrating eye. I had been silent too long.

"I shouldn't dream," I said, "of in any way interfering with the principles on which you run The Roses. I'll co-operate to the best of my ability."

"Thank you, Mrs Grant. I was sure you would understand."

I could certainly undertake to co-operate: but I couldn't answer for Aunt Sophia, who was a strong-minded woman and still remarkably alert mentally. But to my surprise she slipped into the atmosphere of The Roses from the start. The day was skilfully broken up by mealtimes, elevenses and so on. There were cosy little sessions of physiotherapy and occupational therapy—if patients wanted to weave bags, embroider tapestry, they could. Aunt Sophia declined. "I've always hated sewing and I won't begin now." There was a library of light novels, which she read with relish. And a small colour TV by each bed provided some contact with the outside world. The TVs surprised me. Meeting Dr Mactaggart-Thom one day as he admired a splendid bed of roses, I said, "Doesn't the TV distress the patients? I mean the violence and sudden – "

He raised a deprecating hand. "Please, not that word. And 'guests' rather than 'patients'. Hmm? No. TV does not disturb them. To them, it is something quite outside them and not quite real . . . and it fills the day. The great thing is to avoid blank spaces; otherwise they may begin to have unpleasant thoughts. Ah! Here's the car. Excuse me. One of our guests is going back home—a proud moment for us. He was quite convinced that he—that life held nothing more for him when he came. Now he is returning home."

From beside the rose-bed I watched while an old man, walking with a tripod, was packed into a large and shiny car and driven off beside an anxious-faced middle-aged woman. Then I made my way to Sophia's room. Perhaps what I had just seen did justify all the luxury, the cocooning against reality. Perhaps ignoring the facts could be therapeutic. That afternoon I saw Sister.

"Is there any likelihood that Mrs Hope will ever be able to go home? I saw a p—, a guest leaving today."

Sister shook her head. "Not a chance. And Mr Penhurst will be back in a month. They all come back."

I had to admit to myself that Sophia was as happy—if one could use the word about a totally negative absence of unpleasantness—as was possible for

3

a person in her condition. She lived, apparently, from moment to moment, never thinking of the future but lingering among the pleasanter memories of the past. She rapidly built up a strong attachment to her room-mate (there were no single rooms at The Roses; they encouraged "undesirable intro-spection", I was told). I never knew Miss Shivas's first name; following the convention of their time they were always "Mrs Hope" and "Miss Shivas" to each other. She was perhaps not as mentally alert as Sophia—at times she seemed to slip into another time-stream—but physically she was in better shape, did quite a lot of physiotherapy, and could make her way up and down the corridor with the help of a zimmer. She also, I gathered, had a niece who visited her at intervals but our paths never crossed. Aunt Sophia and she seemed to spend a lot of time exchanging reminiscences; occasionally, to their vast content, finding they had common acquaintances at some remote connection. Altogether, I began to feel that Sophia was probably in as satis-factory circumstances as the situation allowed.

Time passed. The rose-beds declined into winter austerity—not shabby, as my roses always looked in winter; it was clear these roses enjoyed every advantage, and were being tended with all the horticultural skill available, to mitigate the disadvantages imposed by the routine of nature. Christmas was celebrated at The Roses with exactly the right note of good taste—a beautiful Christmas tree, holly and evergreens, a suitable present for each guest. Sophia got an amazing number of cards; Miss Shivas very few; I sent her one myself. I learnt with surprise that she was even older than Sophia and must have had few friends left. Her niece sent a magnificent bouquet of out-of-season flowers, which, to my amusement, rather roused the envy of Sophia, who ordered me to send her a similar display at her own expense.

On the other hand, Easter went by unnoticed; not surprisingly, it being difficult to celebrate Easter if you've put a taboo on Good Friday.

One day at the end of May,when I went into Sophia's room, she was not in her bed. Miss Shivas told me she was having her hair done—a hairdresser came regularly to the little hairdressing-room at the end of the corridor—and would be back soon. I sat down to wait and made conversation.

"You're fortunate here in having a hairdresser coming."

"Yes indeed. We are very well looked after." She raised her head from the heaped-up pillows. "Not only all this—waving a thin hand latticed with the prominent veins of old age round the room—but in other ways."

She beckoned me to lean closer.

"Before I came here, I was afraid, *very* afraid. But not any more." Her voice, surprisingly clear for one of her age, dropped; her glance shifted sideways, and she said, softly and clearly but not addressing me, "It happened to the others, but it won't to me, no, never, never to me."

I had seen her have one of these lapses, when it was as if a cog missed and her mental grip on things slipped, and I was going to take her hand and draw her back to reality when Sophia was wheeled in, splendidly blue-rinsed and very cheerful. Sister followed behind; she gave a sharp glance at Miss Shivas, nodded to me and said brightly, "Miss Shivas! Time for your walk", and at once the cog slipped back and the old lady was herself again.

A fortnight later, when I came to see Sophia before going off on holiday, Miss Shivas was progressing down the corridor with two tripods, helped by a physiotherapist and watched by Sister. I paused to watch too.

"Will Miss Shivas be going home soon?" I asked.

Sister looked startled.

"Going home?"

"She seems so much more active."

"Oh, I see. Well, there are problems."

"I suppose it depends on her niece."

"Well, yes, it does rather. And relatives aren't always willing. . . ."

Aunt Sophia was in an unusually morose mood, due entirely to the fact that I was going away for a fortnight.

"Shan't have any visitors," she said. "I've got used to you coming in."

"Oh but you will have visitors," I said, and mentioned a few names. "Besides, you've got your television to look at."

"I never do look at it. All the plays are full of fighting and nasty things. Just put it on and you'll see."

I switched on. It was a news bulletin and the little screen was filled with soldiers with guns at the ready running down a street towards a column of smoke billowing up with slow menace. In the foreground two ambulance men knelt by a woman lying in an ominous sprawl.

"You see," said Sophia petulantly, "that's what I mean. Always something nasty. They shouldn't put on plays like that."

"It isn't a play."

But I said no more, switched off, and talked of other things. As I went out into the sunlight I thought that Dr Mactaggart-Thom would probably be highly delighted with Miss Shivas and Aunt Sophia. The one didn't believe it would happen to her and the other didn't believe it happened to other people. It might be highly satisfactory to the good doctor, but for myself. . . . But I was off on a fortnight's holiday and I was firmly resolved to put The Roses and all it implied behind me.

When I entered Aunt Sophia's room on my first visit after returning, Miss Shivas's bed was empty. After greeting Sophia and handing over the small present I had brought, I said, "Where's Miss Shivas?"

"She's gone home."

"Gone home?"

At first I wondered, but Sophia went on, "Yes, her niece came for her. Quite suddenly, and we didn't get a chance to say goodbye. They had wheeled me into the sun balcony, and when I came back she was gone. But I've had a letter from her. There it is. You can read it."

A sheet of notepaper lay on her locker. I lifted it. It was a grey-blue colour, oddly stiff and with a faint musty smell as if it had been kept for a long time in a damp cupboard. The writing was faint and spidery but legible enough, and the contents were brief. Miss Shivas was sorry she hadn't had time to say goodbye and was missing their nice talks.

"It was nice of her to write," I said.

"Yes it was, and when I feel like it, I'll answer."

Miss Shivas's bed remained unoccupied. I made unobtrusive inquiries and Sister said they found it harder to fill beds owing to having to put charges up. Aunt Sophia certainly seemed to miss the company and I began to see a deterioration in her condition; she was less alert, less cheerful. So I was quite glad when after about a week she greeted me with more animation than she'd shown for some time and said, "I've had another letter from Miss Shivas. There it is."

I took the letter from the envelope. The paper still smelt damp and musty; the writing was even frailer. It was a sad little letter. Miss Shivas didn't feel at home; she had nothing in common with the other people, looked back with regret on her pleasant conversations with Mrs Hope, and would like to think they could meet again. She remained hers affectionately.

"She doesn't seem very happy," I said, as I put the letter back into the envelope. For a moment I wondered what was odd about it.

"The letter isn't stamped, Aunt Sophia. How did it get here?"

"How do I know?" She was unusually querulous. "It was there when I woke up. I expect her niece handed it in."

"Probably, I see she uses the same notepaper as you do, but it must have been in a cupboard for a long time."

"What does it matter? I'm tired. I think you'd better go."

It was then I realised how quickly she was failing. Three days later I got word that she had passed away.

All the arrangements were, of course, made with the utmost tact. When everything was over, I paid a last visit to The Roses to pick up her personal effects. When I arrived there was no one about; the whole place was quite silent with an early-afternoon hush. The guests were all asleep, all lapped in a vast make-believe, carefully cocooned against the last experience available to them. . . . I went up to Sophia's room. The two beds were made up, immaculate; the room a model of airy freshness. Sophia's travelling clock, her silver-backed brushes, her writing case were neatly arranged on her locker. And on top of the writing case, an envelope.

Yes. Another letter from Miss Shivas; unstamped. Her niece couldn't have heard. . . .

I forced myself to open it. The mustiness was even more marked; it was almost an earthy smell: the writing was fainter, in places illegible, but one phrase stood out: *I feel quite lost here.*

Some little sound made me look up. Sister stood in the doorway.

"Oh, good afternoon, Sister. There was no one about, so I just came up."

"That's all right. I think everything is in order."

"Yes indeed. And I'd like to thank you for all the care my aunt enjoyed."

"Well, it's our job, you know. We try to make our guests happy."

"I know. Poor Miss Shivas doesn't seem too happy, now she's gone."

"Miss Shivas?"

I hadn't realised before that Sister must be much older than she appeared. And why was she so white?

"She's written two or three times to my aunt, but they're rather sad letters."

"But she can't have."

"But she has. Here's a letter I found today."

I held it out to her. The earthy smell lingered between us. Sister backed against the locker, her hands raised in rejection.

"She can't have. Miss Shivas is dead; she died when you were away. She's dead; dead and buried."

The forbidden words hung in the air and into their aftermath came a sharp order.

"Sister, you had better go to my office."

Dr Mactaggart-Thom stood aside to let her pass. Then he turned to me. "I'm sorry about that. Sister forgot herself—perhaps she has been doing too much."

I was bundling Sophia's things into the case and didn't answer.

"I am sorry," he repeated.

I looked at him. All I could see were the bones of his skull sharp beneath the skin and the rigid rictus of his smile. I brushed past him and ran down the stairs, through the gleaming silent hall, past the rose-beds, down the drive and back into my world of life and death.

Scotch Settlement

Neil Paterson

1

IT WAS Harry got the picture. At school. The earth was too hard to work in winter and so Harry was goin' to school, and big Andra Jamieson he had the picture, he was allowed books with pictures in his house, he had hundreds, he said, mebbe thousands, he had this picture down the leg of his pants and Harry said, "Give us it." Harry said he said, "Please, Andra." "You don't have to beg," Andra said. "It's yourn." And he gave Harry the picture, and Harry took me down past the clearing to the hemlocks and showed me.

"Mutts," I said.

"No," Harry said. "Dawgs. These are English setter dawgs and mighty rare. Real dawgs."

We looked at the picture. There was two dawgs. One was settin' on his backside and one was on his four legs. The one that was settin' was squintin' up at the one that was standin', an' he was tongue out and rarin' to go. I guess he was grinnin' straight at me. He was the dawg I liked the best of them.

"They're red dawgs," Harry said, "and their picture was took for sellin'. Anybody wants them dawgs he can have them, it says, for twenty-five dollars apiece."

"Is twenty-five dollars a deal of money, Harry?" I asked.

"Twenty-five dollars," Harry said. "Ah, yes."

We looked at the picture for a long time and Harry let me hold it.

"Ain't none of the kids in the whole of Canada belongs a pair of two dawgs like this," Harry said. "I am to call mine Rover. What you goin' to call yours, Dave?"

"I was aimin' to call mine Rover too," I said.

We had a hide-out Harry built down there in the hemlocks at the edge of the water. There was no wet settin' on account of the canoe birch we laid down in strips for floor. We set on the floor of our own two's secret house and looked for a long, long time at the picture of the red dawgs. They sure was pretty.

"There's Gramma hollerin'," Harry said at last.

"I don't hear her."

"You never hear," Harry said. "Come on." He folded the picture and put it in his pocket, and we rolled up my trousers so as my gramma would not see the ends was wet and say, "You been down by the hemlocks again," and then we went on up for our rations.

"Do you know where I aim to hide this picture?" Harry said.

"No," I said.

"In my grandaddy's boots."

I looked into Harry's eyes to see what he meant, and I saw that Harry meant what he said.

"But, Harry," I said. It was no use. Harry could speak faster'n me, and I never yet talked him into anything or out of any other thing. Harry was eight and smart, and I was but four.

"No other place," Harry said, his mind was made up. "Grandaddy's boots."

I thought of my grandaddy's boots and of my grandaddy. I had a bad stomach, thinkin'. "I wouldn't, Harry," I said.

"Safest place," Harry said. "My grandaddy has been to the Convention, and his boots is oiled and on the shelf. Come the spring, my grandaddy will put on his boots and go down to the Houses again, but till the spring there will be no comin' and goin' among people and no need for the boots, and no sich safe place in all the house as the insides of them. You take it from me, Dave," Harry said.

I shook my head. I didn't like it at all. I knew it was two sins. It was a sin to have a picture in the house, and it was a sin to touch my grandaddy's boots. My grandaddy was death on sin. He had eyes sharp as a woodcock for wrong-doin', and when he saw a sin he raised his voice to Heaven and said so, and if it was us had done the sins he took us into the woodshed and beat us. Once he beat Harry justly till he bled. My grandaddy was a just and terrible man. He was bigger'n anybody's door I ever seen except our own, and he'd a bin bigger'n ourn too if it hadn't been he built the hole to fit hisself. He was thick as two towny men put together, and he had a black beard shaped like a spade that he could a dusted the crumbs off the table with by noddin' his head if he had a mind to, which he hadn't. He could not write except for J. Mackenzie, his mark, and he could not read, only some capital letters and the names of God and Jesus and numbers up to 793, which is the end of the Bible, Amen, and he had not any yap like the village men but Conventions, when he sat down Harry said the place where he sat became the top of the table and men pointed their talk at him and kept their traps shut when he opened his. He was a true Christian. He knew God's will, and wreaked it on us.

9

His boots was the best of all the things my grandaddy had, nobody had their like, they was fifteen years old, and he was famed for them. The folks down at the Houses had an idea he wore them boots every day of the year, and they rated him high, Harry said, for this. Folks never guessed that he carried the boots to the outside of the village and put them on behind a tree. Folks did not know that when they came visitin', mebbe once twice a year, my gramma spied them in the valley and beat on the gong and my grandaddy would even come runnin' to get shod before the company arrived. They was black beautiful boots, none of us was ever let touch them, and there was Harry aimin' to hide a picture in them, and pictures was agin God and so was a finger on the boots, and my stomach was jest plain draggin' itself up the track to our house.

My grandaddy was not in the house. You could kinda smell when my grandaddy was in and when he wasn't, not sniff-sniff with your nose, not that kind of a smell, but you could jest smell the nice slack feel of the house.

"Where's my grandaddy?" Harry asked.

"Outside," my gramma said. "Now go and git washed, and hurry, and Davy, you scour them hands. Harry, see he does it."

We came in cleaned and knelt down at our chairs.

"Lord," Harry said, "Father chart hum hum bout to receive hum hum blessed portion hum hum hummy umhum day and night. Amen. Gramma, whereabouts outside is my grandaddy?"

"Amen, Davy!" my gramma said.

"Amen," I said.

"Is he in the woodshed?" Harry said.

"Now pull your chair up afore you set on to it," my gramma said to me. "And never mind the knife. Use that spoon. What was it you was sayin', Harry?"

"I said, where's my grandaddy," Harry said.

"He's had *his* meat a half-hour," my gramma said.

"But where is he? Davy wants to speak to him."

"Me?" I said.

"Your grandaddy is out by the fallen tree," my gramma said. "He's amakin' of fish-hooks. Drink up your goat now, Davy."

"Davy aims to ask him for a dawg," Harry said.

I laid down my spoon and stared at Harry.

"Well, *I* asked last time," Harry said. "Of course, if you're feart to ask."

"I'm not feart," I said.

"Stop gabbin', Davy," my gramma said. "Jest let off gabbin' this instant and eat up your meat."

I ate up and drank my goat. My gramma was for ever pickin' on me, but she had only a little voice—she was small-sized—and meant no harm by it. Although she was small-sized, mind, she was clever. She could weave and, not only, she could read and write, and had spectacles to prove it. She did what my grandaddy said like the rest of us, but once when my grandaddy had me by the pants and there was high words flyin' round my ears, my gramma spoke a piece on her own, and that time it was my grandaddy did what *she* said.

"Gramma," I asked, "why won't Grandaddy let us git a dawg?"

"On account of its rations," my gramma said.

"We could git a little tiny dawg."

"It wouldn't eat but bucket scraps," my brother Harry said. "It would catch all the rats. It'll be a little white rattin' dawg, and we'll call it Rover."

"You'll hev to ask your grandaddy," my gramma said. She took the done dish off the table and went to scrape it in the backyard.

"You finished?" Harry asked.

"Near enough," I said.

"Lord," Harry said. I bowed my head. "Lord hum hum thank God. Amen. Amen, Dave!"

"Amen," I said. "Harry, I never yet seen a red dawg. Did you, Harry?"

"No," Harry said. "But them's red dawgs, sure enough. It says so in the writing. Now go and git down to the tree and ask Grandaddy."

"Okay," I said. "You comin'?"

"No," Harry said.

I went half across the clearing, then I stopped and looked back. "What'll I say, Harry?" I asked.

"Jest say you want a dawg. Go on. There's nothing to be scared of."

When I had gone a little farther Harry shouted, "If he won't let us git a dawg, try him for some other kind of crittur."

"What other kind of crittur?" I asked.

"Any kind," Harry said. It was nothing to him. He was kicking stones round the front door, his hands in his pockets. "Hurry up," he said.

My grandaddy had a fire lit down by the tree. He had got horses' nails off old Neil Munro in the spring, they was the best and softest iron, and my grandaddy knew a way to burn them nails and make them into a steel bar, and then when he had filed a hook on the end of the bar he cut it off, heated it red-hot and tossed it in a bucket of water, and then he picked the hook out of the water and laid it on a hot iron till it was bright blue, and to finish off he dropped it in a fishin'-can full of candle grease, and it got black then, and when it got black it was finished. It was the best and strongest hook you ever seen.

When I got down to the tree my grandaddy was jest cuttin' a hook off the bar. He had his back to me and I could not see, but I knew that was what he was doin' on account of his arm went in and out like a saw. I thought I would wait till he finished cuttin', so I waited. I walked up close, and waited till the hook fell off the bar. My grandaddy had tongs, and he took the hook in the tongs and put it in the fire.

"Grandaddy," I said, "Harry and me wants a dawg."

My grandaddy twisted the hook in the flames and laid it in a red nest in the fire. He had a very black face with the beard, but not his eyes, they was blue and dug right into you.

"Jest even a little mutt," I said.

"What do you want a dawg for?" my grandaddy said.

I could not tell. I knew that we wanted a dawg better nor anything, but I could not jest think what we wanted it for.

"A dawg is no use," my grandaddy said. "You can't eat a dawg."

I could not think of anything to say. I waited a bit, but there was no more talk from him and nothing more comin' from me, and so I went away.

Harry let off kickin' stones and came to meet me. "Well, let's hear it," he said. "What did he say?"

"Said no," I said. "Said you can't eat a dawg."

We walked round to the side of the house without speakin'. We heard my gramma come out the front and start hollerin'.

"Wants you," Harry said.

I looked at the sun. Was my bedtime.

"Harry, I want to be shook if I'm sleepin'," I said, "an' see them dawgs again. Will you, Harry?"

"All right," Harry said. He put up his hands for shoutin'. "He's comin', Gramma!"

I went round the front to my gramma.

"Davy," she said, "was it you hid the scrubber agin?"

I would have said no, but she had a hard face on. "I think it's settin' up there on the kitchen couples, Gramma," I said.

It was tub night. When I was in the tub I told her about my grandaddy. I told her my grandaddy was set agin a dawg.

"Gramma," I said, "I don't like my grandaddy."

"Hush," my gramma said. "Hush now, that's a terrible thing to say. Everybody likes their grandaddy."

"No," I said. "Gramma, Alec Stewart has a grandaddy is on his side."

"Is on his side?" my gramma said, and she left off with the towel.

"Is on his side," I said, noddin'. "Alec Stewart's grandaddy is. He told me."

"Your grandaddy sometimes does not always understand young uns," my gramma said, "and you are too small a young un to understand grandaddies." She rubbed the skin near off me. "Now get shirted up afore I lose patience, and take a great leap into the bed."

I got into the bed.

"If we had a little white rattin' dawg," I said, "it wouldn't eat but rats, and it could have a wee end offa my rations on the Sunday."

"Git over the bed," my gramma said, sharp, "and leave his room for Harry, and stop up all this gabbin' and git to sleep."

"All right. Good-night, Gramma."

"You never can tell," my gramma said at the door. "You might git a dawg some day, Dave. Now git to sleep."

I lay waitin' for Harry.

I could hear next door. I heard my grandaddy come in and grunt, and I heard my gramma, her feet moved round the room, and then she spoke up to him.

"That dawg," she said. "The dawg that Davy wants."

I didn't ketch what my grandaddy said.

"You can't knock man-size sins outa boys that hasn't yit growed up to them," my gramma said. "You own son's sons and you adenyin' them and drivin' them the same wrong road."

"It's God's road," my grandaddy said.

"It's a fool's road, James Mackenzie," my gramma said, "and it ends in cryin'."

Harry came in then, and there was no more talkin' save Harry, he had some gab, and my gramma said yis and no, and Harry came to bed. It was dark, and we couldn't see the picture, and Harry didn't want to talk. He said he was too damn bitter.

"If we *did* get a dawg," he said, "my grandaddy would only eat it."

I lay on my back for a long time. I heard my gramma and my grandaddy git into their bed and I jest lay on, thinkin'.

"Harry," I said. I kicked him. "Would he eat it skin an' all?"

"Eh?" Harry said, he was half asleep. "Eat what?"

"The dawg."

"I don't reckon my grandaddy is truly a dawg-eater," Harry said. "Good-night."

"You don't reckon he would truly eat a dawg?"

"Not a whole dawg," Harry said. "Now shet up and go to sleep."

"All right, Harry," I said. "Good-night."

2

I don't know if it was the next day or some other day, I think it was some other day, the men came to our house. They came ridin' on hosses, and you could see crowds more where they came from, they was without hosses and small as worms way down in the valley. The hosses dug in their heels by our door and the men hollered for my grandaddy.

My gramma put her hand up atop her eyes and took a good hard look at them.

"Where's Jim Mackenzie?" they said. The hosses danced.

"He might be fixin' the fence," my gramma said at last. "Up by the oats."

"Gee-up!" they said. "G'an!" And I ran out from the side of my gramma to watch them go. It sure was pretty to see them hosses calomphin' along, their hoofs hit sparks off the track and the men's backsides jogged up an' down.

"I reckon they came peaceable," my gramma said, "but it don't hurt to make sure. Davy, run down to the wood-pile and tell your grandaddy."

I told my grandaddy and he hit the axe blade into a hardwood log and started for home, and I ran beside him.

"There was guns stuck on the hosses' necks," I said.

My gramma had my grandaddy's boots open for him at the door. "There was five of them, Jim," my gramma said. "One was Joe Cullis."

"Was the hosses sweatin'?" my grandaddy asked.

"No."

My grandaddy laced his boots and took his gun off the top of the door. I ran to git his cartridge belt.

"Thanks, Davy," he said.

We stood watchin' him till he hit the wood and we could not see him any more.

"Will my grandaddy be killin' the hosses too?" I asked.

"Your grandaddy's not agoin' to kill anything," my gramma said, "the idea." But she stayed at the door, listenin', and I was not sure. "You bide by the house now," she said. She took a last hard listen and went in through the door.

Soon I saw Harry, it was his time to be home from school. I gave the scalp whoop and ran across the clearing to meet him.

"Five hosses," I said. "Guns, Guns, Harry, and men ridin' fast."

"That's nothing," Harry said.

"They went calomphin' up to the oats and my grandaddy's git after them. One of the hosses was white."

"Nothin'," Harry said. "Nothin'. Listen, where's grandaddy did you say?"

"He went after the hosses. The hosses was . . ."

"And Gramma?"

"She's in. Harry, my grandaddy's booted up an' he's got his gun."

"Listen, will you," Harry said. "This is *important*. I got somethin' mighty special. You know what I got? Go on, ask me."

"What you got, Harry?" I asked.

"Not so loud," Harry said. "We'll jest ease down the hemlock way like we wasn't goin' nowhere in particler. Hisht now, I got somethin' you wouldn't guess. I got a babby."

"A babby!" I said. "A real babby?"

"Real enough," Harry said. "It's settin' on its hunkers in the hut chawin' away at a root. You feel the weight of it you'd know it was real. I've had it since the mornin'."

"Where'd you git it, Harry?" I asked.

"Found it."

"And is it really ourn?"

"It's mine," Harry said. "But you kin have a loan of it when I got other business. We kin run now."

We ran.

"It's declarin' again," Harry said. "Hear it?"

I heard it plain.

Harry ran on in front, and when I got to the hut he had the babby up in his arms. "Hisht now," he was sayin'. "It had lost its root," he said to me. The babby was dressed in a shawl and long pink pants. Harry set it down and it rolled over and howled. Harry set it up straight and held out the root, and it took the root and shet up and shoved it in its trap.

"Well, doggone," I said. "it's purely real."

"You kin feel it," Harry said, "if you crave to," so I felt it. The babby did not turn its head to look, but its eyes came round the side of the root and gave me a glower.

"Hullo, babby," I said.

It never said nothing.

"Kin it speak, Harry?"

"Ain't exactly gabby," Harry said.

"Is it new-born, mebbe?"

"No, no, it's gittin' on. Listen, Dave," Harry said, "you know what a babby needs best of all. It needs milk. So I aim to go an' tap the goat afore my gramma gits there, an' you bide, see, an' mind the babby. If it drops its root it'll holler, so give it its root back, an' if it still hollers sing to it."

"Okay, Harry." I said.

When Harry was gone I sat down beside the babby and looked at it, and it looked back at me.

"What's your name, babby?" I asked.

It never said nothing.

I poked round it with my finger to see was it well fattened up, and it was. I stroked the top of its head and it never moved, only its eyes, they squinted up; it was jest a young babby and did not know it could not see the top of its own head. It looked hard at its root.

"Tomorra, babby," I said, "I'll cut you a hunk off the old hog. That's better nor root."

I thought I heard Harry, or mebbe it would be my grandaddy. I got a real skeer. I went out and poked my head round the side of the hut, and whenever I went away the babby let out a holler. "Wheesht!" I said. I could not see anything. I went back and said, "Wheesht now!" and when it saw me it stopped hollerin'. It had took a fancy to me. I went away some more times to see would it holler, and every time I went away sure enough it hollered and every time I went back it let off. I reckoned it was some birds I heard. I put my arms round the babby to lift. The babby was willin', but it was plumb solid. I got it up, but my legs had no notion to walk with it. I could of carried it fine on the flat, only them bits of canoe birch was not safe to walk on with a babby. "See," I said, "you're big as me now." I heard a curlew whistle and knew it was Harry, so I put the babby down quick and set it right way up, and Harry came in then. He had a half tin of goat.

"Take the root out of its mouth," he said, "and let me feed it."

I took the root out of the babby's mouth and the babby hollered. It wouldn't look at Harry's tin. It was its root it wanted.

"All right, give it the root to have in its hand," Harry said. He had that babby all weighed off. I gave it the root in its hand, and it shet right up and drank its milk, with Harry holdin' the tin and its face half inside of it.

I laughed to see it drink. "Sure has a thirst," I said.

"One thing about a babby," Harry said, "you got to wet its whistle near every hour of the day. My gramma near ketched me, Dave. I was jest finished at the goat when she came round the side of the house. Look now, you git up for your rations, it's near your time, in case she starts searchin' for you. I gotta wash up the babby an' do its chores."

"And then you'll take it up to the house?" I asked.

"No, no," Harry said. "I aim to keep it in the hut. There ain't nobody but you an me got to know about this babby. It's ourn."

I thought about that. That was good.

"Are we goin' to keep it for ever, Harry?"

"I don't know," Harry said. "We'll keep it here for a year or two anyways, till it's got a mind of its own, and then if it wants to hit the trail, won't be no stoppin' it. Now go on, Dave, up to the house."

I would of liked to bide and watch the baby git its wash, but I had to go for fear my gramma came down by the hemlocks, so I said good-night to the babby and told it I would see it in the mornin', and went on up to the house.

The first thing I seen was my grandaddy's boots.

"Your grandaddy's at the water-shelf," my gramma said, "so say your prayers good."

I said my prayers and ate my rations and drank the wee drop milk that was all my gramma had gotten off the goat, then I said more good long prayers, then my grandaddy came in from the water-shelf and my gramma took me out and scrubbed my hands and face.

"Gramma," I said, "when I was a babby did I have a towel round my middle?"

"You did," my gramma said. "And all babbies has."

"Why?"

"Why?" my gramma said. "So as the babby is all plugged up, of course. A babby is like a cat, you see. It has got to be teched about sich things, jest like a cat or any other young crittur."

"But it's better nor a cat," I said. "Nor a dawg neither."

"Granted," my gramma said. "Now say good-night to your grandaddy and git bedded."

I said good-night to my grandaddy and got into the bed. I clean forgot about the hosses and the guns, I was too busy thinkin' about the babby, the games me and it would play, and what we was goin' to call it, that specially.

When Harry came in I asked him.

"I aint jest settled on a name yet," Harry said, he whispered. "You thought up somethin'?"

"We could call it Rover," I said.

"No, no."

"Rover's a good name, Harry," I said.

"Rover's a dawg name," Harry said. "It's a good name for a dawg, but not for a babby. I had a notion now to call it George."

"George is a good name too," I admitted, "but I like Rover best."

"I tell you t'ain't fitten," Harry said. "And whose babby is this babby anyway?"

"It's your babby, Harry," I said.

"Well," Harry said, "I am goin' to call my babby George after the King, an' that is now its name, an' we will have no more argy-bargy outa you, Dave, that is if you crave to keep friendly with me and my babby."

"I think George is an extra good name, honest, Harry," I said.

We heard my grandaddy say his prayers through the door, and then we heard the bed creak, and we knew that him and her had gotten into it.

"Harry," I said, "how did you know about them wettin' cloths the babby has on round its middle?"

"I remember my mamma with you," Harry said. "I used to help her, and times I did you myself."

I thought about Harry doin' me. I couldn't remember, but Harry remembered near everything that ever happened from the start of him an' me. Harry remembered my daddy and my mamma. He used to tell me pictures of them in bed, and my daddy was a big man in a white shirt, as strong and thick as my grandaddy, but not so hairy and twice as clean, and my mamma was purely beautiful with a soft way of strokin' you and you could tell her anything, and she did a lot of laughin', but never at you, and her face was like in a picture book. Not like my gramma, who was kind, but her face was strictly useful. I asked my gramma about my mamma, but my gramma never liked to look back, she only said, "Your mamma was somethin' special, even if she did marry our Alec. Remember always she was somethin' special, puir lassie; she had hands fine as a lady's."

"What are ladies' hands like, Gramma?" I asked.

"Very clean," my gramma said.

I used to wash my hands sometimes when I was not told, because I wanted to be somethin' special too. I looked at my hands in the dark and I thought about the babby and the babby's hands. The babby's hands was fat and thick and dirty. "Did you wash the babby's hands, Harry?" I asked.

"Wheesht," Harry said. "Yis, I washed it all. I'm goin' now."

I must a been half asleep, lyin' there thinkin', because I saw that Harry was over by the windy and he was dressed with all his clothes on. "I'll be back afore they git up in the mornin'," Harry said, and he climbed right out the windy.

I listened for a long time. I couldn't hear but my grandaddy snorin' and the birds, the noises they made in the wood. I wouldn't be surprised if I heard a wolf too. There was a terrible lot of noise in that old dark wood.

"George," I said. It was a good name right enough, but it wasn't sich a good name as Rover. I put my head under the blankets and went to sleep.

Next day my gramma and my grandaddy thought Harry was at school, but Harry was not at school. Harry was down at the hut with the babby and me. Harry was very sleepy on account of he had been too cold to sleep hardly all night, and so he lay in the hut alongside the babby's nest and slept, and I had the babby to myself. I and the babby had a fine time. The babby had three teeth and a brown spot that wouldn't wash off under its chin. It could stand holdin' on, but it didn't aim to stand on its own. I reckon it was a real lazy kind of babby. It was hard to please with its rations too. It did not like salted ham, and it even did not like a tasty hunk of cheese. It liked water and root, and it wanted to eat a stick of wood, but I did not let it until I had washed the stick good in the lake, and then I told the babby it was jest to sook.

When Harry waked up he sent me to the house for sweet taters, and I got that. Then he sent me to the house for a chunk off my gramma's bolt of cotton, that was for wettin' cloths for the babby, he said to wait till my gramma was out the back, then git the big shears and cut off a hunk this size, he showed me, but I could not work the shears. I got the beginnin' of a hole made, then my hand stuck in the handle of the shears and the blade of the shears stuck in the cloth and I thought I heard my gramma comin', and I picked up the whole bolt and shears an' all and ran; it was bigger'n me that cloth, and it tripped my legs, and I could not see where I was goin', and it got real dirty and scratched with us fallin' and I lost the shears some place and could not find them, but Harry said never mind, my gramma did not see me, nobody did, that was all that signified.

I had to go up to the house for my dinner, and I got some in my pockets for Harry and up my jersey too; my grandaddy was not there, and I did not have to say long prayers, and when I got back Harry had a fire built and the sweet taters was roastin' on the fire. We had ample rations, but the babby was plumb finnicky and would not eat its tater, only a mite when it got cold, and a half slice of bread.

Harry watched the sun. He knew the size of the trees' shadders on the lake, and when they was the right size he said it was time for him to be outa school, and he better had go work a hand on that little old goat afore my gramma, she got there.

"Same as yestiddy, Dave," he said. "It's all yourn till I get back." He meant the babby.

I went and looked to see had he really gone, and then I came back and pulled the babby outa its nest, the babby was hollerin', and set it on my knee.

"Wheesht now, you're my babby now," I said, "Rover."

When Harry came back he was shakin' his head. Wasn't no milk but a little, it was a spoon's fill in the bottom of the tin. "Go up to the house, Dave," Harry said, "and git some pure water for mixin' in." The babby was smart. When it saw the tin it started declarin'. "Hurry, Dave," Harry said, so I went runnin'.

I near run right into my grandaddy.

My grandaddy was standin' in the clearing and a big man along of him. That man was Mister McIver the preacher, and he was the dominie too. He was a true Christian like my grandaddy, he was fierce as a wolf, and his beard was red.

"You! Go git Harry," my grandaddy said, and his voice was small but bad. I turned and ran back into the trees. I ran my fastest to the hut.

"Red Kiver, Harry!" I said. "Red Kiver, the dominie! And my grandaddy wants you."

"Where?" Harry said. "Where, where, Dave?"

"In the clearing." I pointed.

Harry laid the babby in its nest and turned his eyes to Heaven.

"My grandaddy's hoppin' mad," I said, "on account of he must of got ketched with his boots not on. You better hurry."

"Lord sweet God, have mercy on me," Harry said. "A poor sinner."

I took his hand and we went up to the clearing.

"Come here," my grandaddy said. He pointed Harry with his beard. "Here." And Harry went and stood at the end of his beard. "Now," my grandaddy said, "you stand for judgement. Hev you aught to say?"

Harry shook his head, he did not look.

"The boy has sinned doubly. He has been absent two days," the dominie said, and he limbered his arm. "I maun thrash him, Jim."

"Ay," my grandaddy said, "you maun thrash him, John. This is fair an' fitten since you are his dominie, but you will thrash him in the school's time, I say, an' not in mine."

A glare got up between my grandaddy and the dominie, their eyes stuck out like the prongs of forks.

"I came as friend, Jim."

"You kin go as friend, John," my grandaddy said, "if you so please. You spoke as dominie. A man sends his childer to school, the dominie has the use of that childer in school-time. But when the school is out, a man has the use of his own childer and his childer's childer, and on my land an' in my time no man thrashes mine but me. Harry, git to the woodshed. An' you, Davy, go up to the house for your rations."

I went to the house.

"I never called you yit," my gramma said. "What ails you?"

"Nothing," I said. I sat on my stool at the corner of the fire and wisht for a miracle to deliver Harry from the Christians. After a long time my grandaddy came stompin' in, I couldn't look.

"What was John McIver the preacher after?" my gramma said.

"It was John McIver the dominie," my grandaddy said. "He came by with a search party. They is serchin' the upper wood an' he stopped by to query for Harry. Harry has been absent the school two days syne."

My gramma opened her mouth and took that in. "And where is Harry?" she asked.

"In the woodshed."

"Hev you beat him?" my gramma said. Her face was shut up tight, and sour.

"No," my grandaddy said. "That is for the dominie. I have ast Harry where he has been and what he has been doin', but he does not aim to tell me. He defies me, an' so I hev shut him in the woodshed, an' he will bide there until he sees the error of his ways. He will git no rations but water. We will now pray."

After we had et, my gramma gave me a cot's lick at the water-shelf and sent me to my bed. I thought mebbe my grandaddy would go and git Harry, and my grandaddy did go to the woodshed, but he came back single. My gramma spoke for Harry, but my grandaddy hit the table a smack and said, "Silence! I have said he bides, woman. An' bide he will."

It was dark.

I put on my clothes and opened the windy enough to git through. There was more noises than any other night, and the ground was a long way down from the windy and I could not see it. I did not want to go, but I knew somebody had to guard the babby from the wild beasts and give it its feed. I put my legs over and hung by my hands. I hung for a long time. After a bit I thought I would climb in again, but I couldn't. I couldn't let go neither. If my grandaddy hadn't been there I'd have hollered for my gramma. I jest hung by my fingers till they bent up. Then I fell. I wasn't hurt except my fingers was sore and my knees was scraped.

It was awful dark.

If somebody got lost on a dark night like that they'd mebbe never git found for days, and if they went down by the hemlocks they might fall into the lake too. The beasts was prowlin' around the wood, you could hear them, and the birds was screamin' with fright.

I went to the woodshed and shouted "Harry."

I gave a whole heap of kicks on the door and shouted "Harry, Harry, Harry."

"Is that you, Dave?" Harry said.

"It's me," I said. "Harry, I'm not feart. Harry, mebbe I can't find the hut down by the hemlocks an'll fall into the lake. But I'm not feart, not of the wolves neither."

"I can't hear you," Harry said. "Dave, when you git down there, give the babby its drink and change its wettin' cloth. Can you do that, Dave?"

I didn't know could I or not. I was watchin' a square-shaped beast the size of an ox, it was hidden in back of a bush.

"And then," Harry said, "see the babby is warm and tucked low in its nest, and you can top it up with my gramma's cloth too."

"Harry," I said, "and I can't get back in the windy, it's too high. Harry, there's a great big beast out here glowerin' at me."

"There's what?"

"A great big beast," I said. "But I'm not feart."

"Stop screamin'," Harry said. "It don't do any good to scream."

"I'm not screamin'," I said. "I'm not feart, Harry, even if there's two of them. Harry, will it soon be light?"

"No, it won't be light for a long time," Harry said. "Dave, is there truly a beast? Are you awful feart?"

I could hear my heart, and my hair was hot.

"Are you, Dave?"

"Yes," I said. "And I'm feart of the wolves too, and mebbe I'll fall in the lake and I can't git back in the windy and could be I got lost in the wood and never was found again."

"Well, shet up for a minute," Harry said, "and let me think."

I shet up. I never looked near the beast again, but it took a step nearer and breathed on the back of my neck.

"Harry," I said, "are you still there, thinkin'?"

"Yes," Harry said. "Listen, Dave, there is only one thing for it. You are too little to do for the babby. Go on up to the house and tell my gramma. Tell her about the babby needs its milk. Go on now, run."

I couldn't run. I couldn't move.

"Go on," Harry said. "Dave, hev you gone?"

I heard the beast again and I let out a great loud scream. I guess mebbe I thought I would scare that beast away. I jest stood with my eyes shut and the scream kept skirlin' outa me.

"Dave, is that you, Dave? Where are you?" my grandaddy's voice said, and I opened my eyes and saw his lantern.

"Tell my grandaddy!" Harry said. He was shoutin' and hammerin' on the inside of the shed. "That's grandaddy. Tell grandaddy!"

I ran like a tiger and took a leap at my grandaddy's legs.

"It's the babby," I said. "The babby, Grandaddy!"

He picked me up level with his face and I told him. His face was lamp-lit and queer.

"In the hut by the hemlocks," I said.

"Show me," he said.

I took him down by the hemlocks. The beasts was fair feart of my grandaddy and was all runnin' far away. We heard the babby's holler, and my grandaddy put his face to the sound and widened his legs, and I had to run to keep with him.

The babby was crinkled up and red with its holler, but it let off when it saw the lantern. It was okay. I had to laugh, I was that pleased. "It's mine and Harry's, Grandaddy," I told him. "Our babby."

My grandaddy dug his hand under the babby and lifted it, nest an' all, like in a shovel.

"And that's its milk," I said. "In the tin."

My grandaddy went out the door of the hut and up through the hemlocks towards the house. I was behind and I could not see. I kept fallin'. I ran fast as a hoss, but there was little trees I could not see, and I was scratched an' bleedin' and times I fell in the marsh, and I could not ketch my grandaddy.

"Grandaddy, what are you goin' to do with it?" I cried.

He never said nothing.

"Wait for me, Grandaddy," I said.

But he never waited, no nor spoke.

I got feart all of a sudden. I was very, very feart. "It's mine and Harry's," I shouted. "It's ourn!"

In the clearing I fell too, but I could run faster then and I ketched him up. I clawed at his leg, but his leg was movin' and I fell.

"It's ourn," I said. "Ourn."

My grandaddy pushed open the door and went in the house, and I fell on the step and was too tired and sad to git up. I jest lay screamin'. "Don't eat it, Grandaddy," I said. "Tain't fitten. Please, please don't eat it."

My gramma ran and picked me up and rocked me in her arms like I was a babby myself. "There ain't nobody goin' to eat it," she said, "or harm a hair of its mite head. Your grandaddy's going to give it back to its rightful owners, and that is all."

"But it's ourn," I cried. "It's mine and Harry's!"

"Hush now," my gramma said, "it's the Donaldson babby, must be. It's been lost two days, an' all the folks from the Houses searchin' for it, an' its mamma an' daddy near demented."

My grandaddy took the babby to the Houses, and that same night the men came for Harry. They came on hosses. They was hard-faced men, and they stood in a crowd inside the door.

"It's the law," they said.

My gramma kissed Harry and buttoned his coat.

"You'll take good care o' him?" she asked.

"He won't come to no harm along of us, ma'am," they said. "The mob won't git him."

And then they set him on a hoss and took him away, and the next day but one they tried him.

4

The store was the court. There was a big space in the middle of the store, and it was all filled up with folks settin' on benches, there must a been twenty there, and my grandaddy and me sat on the front bench. It was Mister Cameron's store, so it was Mister Cameron's court, Tom Cameron, and he sat on a high chair behind the counter, and a writer next to him. The writer was from up the river.

Harry had a chair to hisself.

A skinny man in black cloth got up on his feet. He was hairless and a stranger, and he began the gab.

"The case for the Crown," he said. "'Duction of young female." Sometimes he pointed at Harry. He spoke for a long time and folks humphed on their seats and scraped their boots; he spoke quiet and used long words; he was not worth listenin' to. "The Crown rests," he said, and sat down.

"Accused," Tom Cameron said.

Sam Howie, standin' back of Harry, poked him with his finger and Harry stood up.

"Harry Mackenzie, you got anythin' to say?" Tom Cameron said.

"The Lord have mercy on me," Harry said. "I am eight years old and a sinner, but I aimed at no harm."

"You understand," Tom Cameron said, "this is your defence. Is that all you got to say?"

"Yes, mister," Harry said.

"*Sir*," the writer said. "You call the court *sir*."

"Yes, mister," Harry said.

Sam Howie poked him with his finger again and Harry sat down. That was the best thing of all. That was right smart. Every time Sam Howie poked Harry he stood up, and if he was standing he sat down. I grinned to Harry, but he was feart to smile back on account of my grandaddy. My grandaddy was settin' with his arms folded and his beard up. He never moved a half inch.

"Well, then," Tom Cameron said, "this is how it looks to me. First, this female child has not come to a deal of harm. That's right, Bill, isn't it? Where's Bill Donaldson?"

"I'm here," Bill Donaldson said, and he stood up. He was the babby's daddy. "Ain't harmed none far as me and my missus can see. Got to admit that."

"Well, then," Tom Cameron said, "on the other side nobody can't deny there's been too much of this particler kind of lawlessness hereabouts. Take last month only. Willie Fleming's daughter. It was that trapper from your way, it was up the river, what was his name, Arch?"

"Foster," the writer said.

"That Foster," Tom Cameron said. "We all know what he did. He had Willie's Sarah off in the woods for twelve days afore the law caught up on him. Well, then we made him marry her right here in this court, and Sarah's got a man and tied up regler and Willie's well pleased, admitted; still an' all, this abductions and crimes has got to cease."

"Sex crimes," the writer said.

"That's right," Tom Cameron said. "Sex crimes too. Our women rate high with us in this community and, rightly, a woman's purity is a hangin' matter. It was time we showed the wild elements that this is so, and a man tampers with womenfolk gits his just deserts."

There was a kind of soft growl from most everybody, and Tom Cameron nodded right and left and pointed to Harry. "Well, then," he said, "we got here a boy who is guilty of the kidnap and abduction of this young female Margaret, daughter of Bill Donaldson. He says he aimed at no harm, and according to Bill he did no harm, but he admits to kidnap, and that is a hangin' crime and has caused a deal of worry to Bill Donaldson and his missus."

"Darn right," Bill Donaldson said.

"Well, now," Tom Cameron said, "we do not aim to be hangin' an eight-year-old boy, and the clerk says they will not take him upriver in the prison, but I hear there is schools for young uns where they can be teched to be reformed, and it is my opinion that we should conseeder the sendin' of Harry Mackenzie to one of them reform schools. Does happen anyone in the court knows aught of them schools?"

My grandaddy stood up and looked round the court, face to face. Nobody spoke, and then my grandaddy looked at Tom Cameron. "If you send him to a school, Tom," my grandaddy said, "I'll shoot you."

"Sit down, Jim," Tom Cameron said, "and don't interfere with the course of justice."

"Contempt of court," the writer said.

"You shet up," my grandaddy said, "you scribblin' Pharisee. As for you, Tom, you know me well, an' you hev my meaning." And he sat down.

"Well, now," Tom Cameron said, and he clucked in his throat and blinked like a little fat owl. "We was saying. I take it nobody here knows aught of them schools?"

"I could find out," the writer said.

"So you could," Tom said. "So you could. You will notice, Jim, that I did not say we was goin' to send the boy to a reform school. All I said was, did anybody know aught of them schools so as the court could conseeder them. Well, now, it seems to me that the cause of justice would be served if the Clerk here was to find out all about them reform schools and then the court will have the information it needs and can send Harry Mackenzie to a reform school if it thinks fit the *next time* he appears on a similar charge. Case dismissed. That's all today, folks."

Sam Howie poked Harry with his finger and Harry stood up. "You're let aff," Sam said.

Everybody got up, started movin' and speakin'. "Store's now open," Tom Cameron said, shoutin'. "Anybody aims to buy."

"Harry," my grandaddy said, "come here."

Harry came.

"Hullo, Harry," I said.

He never spoke or looked at me. He was white as sickly and his eyes was set low.

"Take Davy home," my grandaddy said. "Git straight home, the both of you, and you Harry set on your chair and wait there till I get home. Do you hear me?"

"Yis," Harry said. He whispered.

"Git movin' then," my grandaddy said.

Harry took my hand and we went home.

"You feelin' okay, Harry?" I asked.

"Yis," Harry said. "But there is an awful thing happened. Dave, you guess what's happened? My grandaddy got his boots on, and you know what is in the inside of them boots. It was the left boot."

I stared at him. I had clean forgot.

"The picture," Harry said. "The picture of the dawgs."

"Ah God," I said.

"So I will git two thrashings," Harry said. "Thrashed on account of the babby and thrashed on account of the picture."

"Mebbe I will git thrashed too," I said.

We went straight but slow.

"If he beats me till the blood comes," Harry said, "I am goin' to run away. Happen there is bits of my behind that I cannot see myself, so you will look for me, Dave, and if there is blood shows I will run away."

"I will run away too, Harry," I said.

"I am not goin' to stay and be beat to death," Harry said. "If he bloods me I will truly run away."

"Me too," I said.

I thought about runnin' away. I wondered where we would run to.

"Harry," I said. "That babby. It was a girl babby."

"Yis," Harry said. "Kin you walk faster, Dave?"

"Me? Easy," I said.

"Well," Harry said, "we better."

We walked fast. I thought of the places I knew. We could not run away to the Houses on account of we would only git ketched, and we could not run away to the woods on account of there was only beasts in the wood and there would be nobody to give us our meat.

"My gramma is makin' a pie," I said.

"What kind?" Harry asked.

"I forgit."

"Was it a berry pie?"

"I purely forgit," I said. "Harry, mebbe my gramma would run away with us too. That would be fine, wouldn't it, Harry?"

"No," Harry said. "She is on his side."

"My grandaddy spoke up for you in the court," I said. "He was on our side then, Harry."

"Yis, of course," Harry said. "But that is with strangers. Him an' her is on the same side in the family. You tell my gramma a word of this about runnin' away and I will not take you with me. I mean that, Dave."

"All right," I said. But I felt sad. "I won't tell, I swear it, Harry."

We got to the house and went in.

"So you're home," my gramma said. "And hongry, I'll be bound."

"No, I ain't hongry," Harry said.

"Ain't hongry!" my gramma said. "I never. Well, I know somebody that is."

"Me neither," I said.

"I got a pie. Blackberry pie."

"I ain't hongry, Gramma," Harry said.

He sat down on his chair at the corner of the fire and I sat on my stool. My gramma stood starin'.

"We're waitin' for my grandaddy," I said. "My grandaddy said set and wait for him."

"Oh," my gramma said. She wiped her hands on her apron and shut her mouth up tight, and after a minute she turned to the skillet.

We waited a long time.

My gramma put the knives and tools on the table. "Even though you ain't hongry," she said, "you jest had better eat."

"Listen, there's my grandaddy!" Harry said.

I listened.

"Hear him?" Harry said. Harry was begun to shake, and me too, my knees was jiggin'.

My grandaddy opened the door and my gramma slammed the pie on the table. She stood and stared, jest stared.

"You sold them, then, you really did it!" she said. I looked where she was lookin', and saw that my grandaddy was barefit, "You walked through the Houses in your bare feet, Jim!"

"They are clean," my grandaddy said. "My good name is in God's hands and my pride does not rest in ornaments. Harry, git your gramma the quill and parchment."

Harry's hands was not trusty. He dropped the quill on the floor and I ran and picked it up.

"He will write it his own self," my gramma said. She spoke firm. "Harry will."

My grandaddy did not argue.

"Sit down, Harry," my gramma said.

My grandaddy plucked a paper outa his pocket and laid it on the table. Harry began to cry. I never seen Harry cry in all my life before. I looked at the paper. It was the picture of the dawgs.

"Take up the quill an' write," my grandaddy said. "Write this: 'Sir, I here enclose $26.50 for one red setter dawg and carriage of same stop in good condition and oblige.' Hev you writ that?"

Harry shook his head.

"Well, write it," my grandaddy said.

"And add this," my gramma said. "Yours in good faith." She was smilin' pretty as a young mamma, and she spoke slow and proud. "Yours in good faith," she said. "James Mackenzie."

Harry wrote like fury; my grandaddy leaned over to see every scratch, and my gramma put her hand on my head.

"We're goin' to git a dawg," I said. "Are we, Gramma?"

"Yis," she said, smilin'. "Yis, Davy."

"I reckon we'll call it Rover," I said. "Eh, Harry?"

Harry looked up for a minute and nodded, grinnin', and my grandaddy nodded too. "Rover's a right enough name," he said. I stood close up with my chin on the table, watchin'. I was mighty content, not only on account of the dawg, but on account of I now knew ours was a good family, not like some. In our family we was all on the same side.

Spud: Suffering through Sunday

William Grant

O N THE top landing of a grey Glasgow tenement—constructed for the exclusive purpose of being a slum seventy years past, it had in no way relinquished its position—Beenie moved around the small kitchen in the constrained bursts of laboured activity she had grown accustomed to since passing her sixth month of pregnancy. The least movement seemed to require an effort of will equal to that she had always thought would be necessary for climbing Ben Nevis, which, although she had never personally seen it, filled her imagination whenever anything larger than the hills surrounding the city was mentioned.

What little furniture there was reflected the fashion of the previous decade. Two large armchairs, well worn: a table in the centre of the floor with four matching chairs; a wardrobe, a tallboy, a Welsh dresser and, looking strangely alien, her one concession to contemporary times—a large, expensive, colour television. At this moment, at thirty-four years of age, she felt as old as the building itself. And, to add to her troubles, she could hear him stirring behind the heavy curtains that served to screen off the recessed bed.

Further effort was now demanded. She waddled clumsily towards the stove. Lit the gas-rings. Put on frying-pan and kettle. The bed creaked again; she endeavoured to hurry but could gain no more speed. Mushrooms, tomatoes, eggs, ham, she managed all of them into the pan, nauseated by their stench. Wanting to vomit but strongly repressing the urge in the firm knowledge that, since she had eaten nothing, she would spend an interminable period stooped over the sink retching.

Spud pushed aside the curtains and peered through into the daylight. "How's the time?" he croaked.

"Your breakfast is on," she replied. It having been some years since they had actually listened to each other with anything resembling intent interest.

"How's the time, I said?" He glanced about, his heavy eyes and tousle-haired head disembodied by the curtains. "Is there any beer left, what's goin' on inside my skull you wouldnae believe?"

"Hell mend you," Beenie muttered indifferently. "Get out of there till I get that bed spread, suppose somebody was to come in, you layin' there at this time of day!"

Since no one would have considered coming in this early on a Sunday morning the question was given the lack of response it seemed to deserve. Pouring out a pint mug of tea she handed it to him. An arm extended cautiously to join the head. He swallowed a mouthful, delighting in his agony as the scalding liquid seared the roof of his mouth.

"Where are the weans?" he questioned.

"Up and oot afore eight. Just have a gander at it, the sun's splittin' the chimney-tops—lazy bugger!"

Spud directed his gaze towards the window but could see nothing but a brilliance that pained his eyes. "Is that ham I smell . . . ?"

"Are you getting up like I asked?" Again she moved laboriously. "Get a move on and use the sink, I want tae get some clothes steeped."

He moved, then paused. His brain seemed to slosh about with an uncontrollable liquidity. The linoleum floor was cold. Unsteadily, he managed the sink. Anguished, the single, brass, swan-necked tap gushed forcefully. The water looked extremely frigid—threatening.

"Stop looking at it as if it was going to eat you," Beenie frowned.

Plunging his head under the downfall he roared, unable to restrain himself. It served its purpose, however; his system was instantly wrenched from its lethargy, adrenalin surged into his blood. He laughed, enjoying the sense of release, and put his arm around her from behind, grasping her milk-firm breast. "How's about a kiss then?"

"Get off!" she said, pushing his hand away. "You're no' two minutes wakened."

"I'm jist right in the mood. I woke up hours ago dyin' for it."

"If you don't let me get your breakfast oot o' this pan it'll be burned tae a frazzle!" When he persisted she brushed her lips along his cheek. "There now, give me peace."

"Is that it?" he asked in the hurt tones of a child.

Beenie glanced at him tiredly. "Was last night no' enough?"

Spud looked surprised. "I don't think it could have been. Did I enjoy myself?"

"You want to be on the receiving end one of these times, there's nae living wi' you when you've got a drink in your head." Instinctively, her hand tested the purple swelling upon her face.

"Whit happened?" he demanded, looking at it with interest, his protective instincts aroused.

Turning off the heat beneath the pan she stood gazing at the contents, containing her anger. "Have you no' heard, we had a visit frae the fairies last night, you know, the green people, the wan that did this had tackety boots on!"

"You must have deserved it," he muttered, recognising his error, still dull-witted with the drink. Had he remembered doing it he would simply have avoided the subject as they usually did.

"It's over and done with," she replied indifferently, "let's just forget it. . . . Sit doon."

"I'll just away for a pee first." Swiftly he exited out of the front door. She heard him running down the single flight of stairs and banging the door of the stairhead lavatory. Her gaze remained fixed upon vacancy. She was well aware of the ploy. Only a further argument which put her in the wrong would ease his guilt. He wanted to sit down there in the cold cubicle on the landing and return to find his breakfast burned.

Beenie performed a frantic search. Her tranquillisers were gone. "Damn, blast and bloody hell!" she uttered, this being the most daring expletive she had ever had the courage to voice.

Spud returned. She now had further ammunition. "Where are they?"

"Where's whit?"

"You must have moved them," she ranted. "God, a house no' the size of a dug kennel and I can never find nothin'!"

His breakfast was on the table. Caught momentarily off-balance he sat down and forked some into his mouth. "This is – !"

"Where are they!" she demanded loudly.

Deciding, in his weakened condition, to settle for a draw he continued to chew. He had wished a victory only if it required little effort.

Beenie, however, found herself ill-suited by the silence. Objects, lifted and searched, were returned heavily to their original positions. The atmosphere grew taut.

"You're runnin' about there like a nun in a brothel huntin' for the door!" Spud reacted. "Whit is it till I get some peace?"

"You know fine well," she challenged. "My pills!"

"Did you look in your other pocket?"

Certain of victory she plunged her hand into the folds to prove him wrong. "How did they manage to get in there?" she asked with genuine surprise, extracting them. Too astonished to register disappointment.

"Two of they things an' you have a struggle tae remember whit time of day it is, much less where you put them!" he frowned. "Fill up my mug, will you?" He extended the mug in her direction.

Beenie accepted this as it was intended, as a sign that by mutual agreement the intended hostilities could now be satisfactorily brought to a denouement. One pill was the dose, she swallowed two. Each hour having to be clambered through in a body unfit for human habitation, these pills were proving her salvation. She filled his mug. "You near finished?"

He nodded. "It was better than it looked."

"Do us a favour then?"

"Depends?"

"Get out of my sight till these things start workin', I'm fair jumpin' inside." She spoke with a hint of concern which held a plea for the continuance of the frail bond that existed between them. Minute as it was they had little else. . . .

"I'll away doon for the papers."

She nodded thankfully. "You'll be goin' for a pint later on, I suppose?"

Surprised, Spud displayed it. "It's Sunday, I always go tae the club on a Sunday?"

Beenie filled the sink with clothes and then poured in some biological detergent. "I just want to talk to you beforehand, that's all."

"Talk away, I'm all ears!" There was caution in his tone.

"Later, we're neither of us in the mood right this minute. It will keep." With this she made her way laboriously over to the recessed bed where, with the aid of the brush-pole as an extension of her arm, she made a vain attempt to spread the covers.

"How's about a kiss afore I go?" Despite the truce he felt the need to have her comply.

Her fury was held down by the dull edge of her soreness. Internally she strangled the scream that had been forcing itself upwards. Instead, she spoke with a firm quietude. With what she had to request of him later on she could not afford this anger. "I'll keep it in mind for when you get back."

Spud could not see her face but accepted the tone as being promise enough. "Right, I'll away then." He exited swiftly.

"And shut the door," she called. But when she glanced up she saw that, as always, he had left it ajar. The draught of it chilled the room.

Enclosed within the rectangle of worn tenements Hammy and Angus played in the dirt of the back court. It had not rained for three days but the pitted holes around the back closes still held large puddles. Nine-year-old Hammy waded through one of their shallows. Angus, who was almost five, circled its perimeters with caution. "Mammy will murder you," he warned.

Hammy shrugged, experiencing a glimmering of fear but relishing the emotion and then pretending indifference. "My shoes will be dry again by the time we go up." He splashed on, proud of his defiance and chanting:

> Mary had a little lamb,
> Her faither shot it deid,
> And noo it goes to school wi' her
> Between two chunks of breid!

He felt stronger than all of the world at this moment. Unlimited. Emerging from the water he squelched his shoes pleasantly against the earth.

"Wish I was at school," Angus bemoaned, knowing that chants such as these were to be learned there.

They sauntered along, bored. With its crumbling brick midden-shelters, each containing three inadequate bins that overflowed, twisted steel clothes-poles, and the remnants of what had once been a line of steel fences separating each allotment, the back court was too devoid of life to hold any interest for them.

"Look!" Hammy roared with an exaggerated enthusiasm, "A rainy-beetle!" With a dash he stepped on it, squashed it flat, then spat and inter-mingled both spit and blood with the point of his shoe. "Bets it rains afore tea-time?" he challenged.

"Is that right, Hammy?" Angus looked upon his brother with respect and awe. "You know an awfy lot of things!"

Hammy nodded, accepting the statement as the truth he knew it to be. He did know a lot of things. Magic things. There were times when he surprised himself with what he knew.

Spud entered from the opposite side of the enclosure, exiting from the end of a close and making towards the rear of his own. Carefully folded in his pocket were the *News of the World* and *The People*.

"There's Da!" Hammy shouted, exhilarated by this promise of instant relief from the dreadful realms of boredom.

"Hallo you pair, nothin' to do with yourselves?" Spud questioned.

The boys laughed, suddenly alive.

"Lift me under the oxters an gie me a swing?" Hammy begged. Dancing about, unable to be still.

"Get away," Spud replied. "You weigh a ton."

Hammy giggled in disbelief, knowing his father to be capable of anything.

Without a further word, but issuing a relenting sigh, Spud lifted his son under the armpits and began to swing him around. Instantly, the blood rushed to his head. He swayed dizzily, was overwashed by nausea, and was forced to stop.

"That wasnae a real shot?" Hammy groaned.

"Me, me next?" Angus shouted, extending his arms.

"Naw," Spud waved them off. "I'm no' fit this mornin'. Christ, that nearly did me in." He breathed heavily. Disappointment filled him, he felt that he had let his son down.

"No' fair," Angus sulked. "He always gets everything, he does."

Spud grinned and nodded. "Right enough," he stated proudly, "but then he's the wan that's goin' to grow up tae be like his faither, right, Hammy?"

"Too true I am, Da!"

Conspiratorially, father and son grinned. This special rapport they accepted as natural to the exclusion of all else, it rendered up a fulfilling warmth.

"I'm telling my mammy if I don't get a swing!" Angus threatened.

They each looked in his direction with something akin to disdain.

"It's a thick ear you'll be gettin'," Spud replied. Then—disruption he did not want—considered what Beenie's response might be, balanced it against the promise of earlier on and drew some soothing coppers from his trouser pocket. "Here, the pair of you, away and buy yourselves some sweeties."

"Dead gemmie!" they shouted in ecstatic unison. Hammy, however, was reluctant to forfeit his father's presence for some dubious delight that, now with money safely in hand, could be gleaned at a later date.

"Is it no' right that you earn lots of money, Da?" he prompted.

With a caution inbred of the hunted, Spud paused before answering, "Well, you know. . . ?"

"I was tellin' my pals!"

"Aw. . . ." Spud grinned with some relief. "I make enough. Aye, don't you fret about that, and I bow to no man for it neither!"

"It's you that tells the daft gaffer an' all the rest o' them what to do, isn't it?"

"If they come tae me for a bit of advice, I give it to them," Spud replied modestly. "I mean, education's all right and that, but it canny replace good common sense."

"Remember when the engineers an' everybody else were lost and you sorted it all oot for them, tell Angus, Da?"

Spud shuffled with embarrassment. "Jist forget about that, eh. . . ? You go on and on about things like that, them things are jist between you and me, right!"

"Right, Da . . . "Hammy replied, downcast.

They felt awkward with each other, a fractured limb no longer able to transpose this sudden, unwarranted gap.

"We've got a bladder in the close?" Hammy offered.

Spud moved his feet awkwardly against the hard dry earth, torn between his need for stability and silence and the loyalty due to his son. An image of the room and kitchen filled his imagination, Beenie predominant. He experienced a surge of desire that was both deep and demanding and wondered if perhaps she had lied to him about last night.

Witnessing his father's dilemma Hammy further prompted. "Just a wee game, jist for a minute. . . ?"

Spud again glanced towards the close and then back to his son. "Aw right, but jist for a minute mind?"

"I bags being in goal!" Angus chimed.

In anticipation of what was to follow all three of them generated excitement.

"This is the goal," Angus informed, pointing from one marker against the rear of the building to another.

Hammy returned with the ball. Handing it to his father, giving him the honour of the first kick. "Bets you canny get it past me?" he taunted, laughing himself at the absurdity of such a statement.

"You're daydreamin'!" Spud retorted playfully. "When I kick the ball you'll no' even be able to see it!"

"I will," Angus bobbed in his goalmouth. "I'll save it."

All three hesitated, as though by some unconscious command, and breathed deeply. With a flurry, the game began. Spud, swerving exaggeratedly, moved past Hammy and sent the ball, with all his force, soaring between the appointed goal-posts. With a loud crack it rebounded off the wall and high into the air. Angus crouched low against the dirt with his hands protectively covering his head.

"Goal!" Spud roared. "Some goal, eh. . . ? Did you see that goal?" he appealed, then reflectively: "When I think o' the mugs who are gettin' paid a fortune for the likes o' that. I could beat any wan o' them wi' wan o' my legs sawn off!"

"Again," Hammy shouted. "That was a smasher, Da." Then goadingly lest his father should consider departing, "Bets you couldnae do it again?"

"Who couldnae. . . ?"

"That was too hard," Angus complained sullenly. "It's no' fair when you hit so hard, I'm no' playin' if you do. . . ."

After inspecting the pots on her range, Beenie added a pinch of salt to the potatoes. She was brighter, now that the pills had taken their effect. Also there was the unaccustomed solitude—a rarity. Her confidence had expanded. She had already worked out the approach she would adopt with Spud, and was fairly confident of its success.

At that instant Spud entered. "I'm back, hen!" he shouted unnecessarily. "I've brought thunder and lightning with me!"

The boys giggled at the suggested notoriety.

She remained with her back to him so that he might not see the anger in her expression. "You were only supposed to be goin' for a paper and right back?" she accused. His extended absence seemed to belittle her present condition.

"So?"

"Did you have to bring them up wi' you, the dinner's no' near ready?"

"Faither said we could come," Hammy interjected defensively.

"We were playin' fitba'," Angus informed. "I was in goal."

Their voices, usually a pleasure to her, gnawed painfully at her inner ear. She experienced a need to burst into tears or scream or to be excessive in some way in the vague hope that it might serve to relieve this sickening lethargy. She seemed incessantly barbed by emotional and physical harpies.

"Haw, aye, jist wanted me myself, eh. ˙. ?" Spud grinned, miming the facial signals of a deep sexual rapport that had long since become etiolated.

Beenie turned around, acting out the game, returning the signal. It was one of their many unconsciously agreed rules of equitable survival. "Aye, jist you." Her voice was pliable and her smile radiant.

Considering her response over-large Spud sensed danger. Instantly he manufactured a little anger to avoid it. "You're not on!" he informed her forcefully. "Whatever it is you're after the answer is no—N.O."

33

"I havenae even said yet. . . ?" Beenie smiled, still playing coy.

Spud was definite. "If you're offerin' that much, that easy, then I canny afford it, it's as simple as that!"

"Jist two lousy pounds!" Beenie rushed out, deciding that only a frontal assault had now any opportunity of success.

"This week?" He was incredulous. "The now. . . ?"

"This week, every week, a rise. Go on, I know you could manage it if you tried?" She kept her tone low and weak, submissive, then added instinctively, "One thing about you, you always look after your family, no' like some others I could mention."

The directness of the request caught him off-balance. He flustered. "Woman, if I had two quid I'd arrange to have it framed as the eighth wonder o' the world!"

"Mammy," Hammy intervened, "can Angus and me have a chocolate biscuit?"

"Your faither an' me's talking," she snapped, dreading any opportunity for digression.

"Jist wan. . . !" Hammy moaned, drawing out his voice.

"You," Beenie glared at him, her husband's favourite. This minor retaliation intimating of others to follow if her ill-favour be gained. Her husband, not the child, the target. "I'll wring your neck if you don't be quiet!"

Spud received the message. He was reminded of the heights her wrath could attain, and of the thousand deprivations that were hers to inflict. "It's jist not possible," he pleaded, but recognised doubt in his own voice. "You'll jist have to cut down on other things."

"Where? I've got two boys to buy clothes for." She sensed victory.

"They get new clothes nearly every week, woman, they're ruined!"

"Aye, and they're goin' to stay that way. What we didnae have they're goin' to get. My weans arenae goin' to go through what the likes of us went through. Are you goin' to start denyin' your ain family for the sake of a few extra pints? Naw, no' you, I don't believe it!"

All three faces were now trained upon him, attempting to determine his response to this accusation. Confronted by them he realised that he, if his present position was to be maintained, had no other option but to relent. The present housekeeping money he did give her was more than sufficient, almost one-and-a-half times what his mates gave their wives, but he could afford another two. In fact, he would profit from it. Until now he had been avoiding Sunday work, unable to commit himself either way. Actually he was pleased now that the decision had been taken for him.

"There's some Sunday work goin'," he said, maintaining his voice at the crushed level of martyrdom. "I'll still have Saturday afternoon off." Internally he felt it to be something of a victory. His own folding money would be increased considerably and he had, to all appearances, openly immolated himself. Beenie was frowning; before the children she had deprived him of his only day off. Spud waved away all protestations before any were attempted.

"My decision, my choice!"

Beenie, aware that if she had considered the possibility of Sunday work she could have asked for as much as five pounds and in all probability gained it, was now forced to accept what she had requested. The confrontation, however, was over. A seasoned campaigner, she accepted defeat, assured of future victories. "You're jist a big darlin'!" she exclaimed, actually quite proud of him for having emerged the victor, and kissed him on the cheek with genuine warmth. Each unsure of what the other was intimating (since the initial action had been entirely spontaneous), they were reluctant to offer less of themselves in case it should be accepted as a slight and encourage hostility. Their arms encircled each other with cautious enthusiasm.

"Two fatty bellies!" Hammy laughed as he witnessed their awkwardness, protruding his own stomach to match.

Spud, over-conscious of his beer belly, broke off, hesitated, then initiated a game by grasping at his son's stomach. "No' as fat as yours, let me feel."

Delighted, Hammy feigned resentment. "Get away!" he giggled, bumping against the table. Spud followed, upsetting one of the light chairs in his eagerness. Beenie allowed it to continue for as long as she could bear. Each additional collision and squeal sent an ever-enlarging shock wave resounding harshly against the raw inner dome of her cranium. Allowing for its present fragility she felt that it was about to rend and permit her vacillating brain to explode free and tear the life from her.

"Enough!" she screamed, only seconds later recognising the voice as her own. She had not wanted to scream and regretted the antagonism it might allow.

They paused. Then stopped. "His fault," Spud said brightly, panting to regain his breath. "Cheeky wee sod."

"Your fault!" Hammy challenged, wishing to continue.

"Jist you dare!" his mother warned. Extracting a pound note from her purse she handed it to her husband. "Here, since the pair o' you have that much spare energy then yous can run back down the stairs and fetch me a wee bag o' coal."

"Ach, Beenie . . ." Spud groaned, "I've only jist come up."

"A cup o' tea will be waiting by the time you get back," Beenie stated, no longer listening.

Resigned, Spud turned to Hammy. "Right then, it's a race, you and me!" And with this he went off through the door with a clear advantage.

Hammy squealed and then followed, leaving a vacuum.

Once again the room became a haven. Clearly not wishing to be disturbed, Angus was squatted in the corner, silently at play. Beenie glanced. She had a fear of late and it now nagged at her. She found herself inadvertently antagonising him. As now, at peace, she could not restrain herself from entering his private sphere in the hope of reclaiming him into her own.

"Whit's the notion of playin' way across there?" she asked cheerfully.

He did not reply. She returned to her chores, wanting to leave him alone.

Inventing self-occupying tasks. She rubbed at the furniture and dusted the mantelpiece unnecessarily.

"Did you no' hear?" she insisted, damning herself for having done so.

"Playin'," he replied, quietly, reluctantly.

She attempted gaiety. "Did you say playin', playin' at what. . . ?"

"Playin'," he answered sullenly. A deliberate, quite unmistakable rebuff.

Suddenly, blindly, irrationally, she experienced the impulse physically to injure him in retaliation for the pain he was inflicting in depriving her of his immediate love. The guilt following this awful reaction only suffused her with an even greater passion. Her need of his love and good opinion was insistent to the exclusion of all else. Each instant she found it necessary to fight to contain herself, to remain an adult for fear of frightening him by rushing to overwhelm him with unrestrained passion.

"You always used to sit on my knee when naebody else was in," she accused.

He refused to reply. She ventured tentatively. "Is it because you don't like me any more?"

The question was stupid to a child, she realised it. Yet, paradoxically, she felt that this alone might be the one concrete truth. In her present condition she felt incapable of being truly loved. Undeserving. A biological monstrosity. She fully realised that others had no way of feeling the vibrant glow of internal life that served to sustain her.

He whispered something.

"Whit?" she rushed out in desperation.

"Nothin' . . ."

"Come on, whit was it you said?"

"Fatty belly," he whispered.

"Still canny hear you," she said, inching hopefully closer.

For an instant he remained silent. Then spat out, "Big, horrible fatty belly!"

She was astounded. "Whit?"

"Are so . . ." he replied unrelentingly. "No' play boxin'."

Beenie recalled the incident. "But I canny let you hit my stomach now – " she began, then realised that there was nothing further to be said. The extent of her quandary was revealed to her. She did, instinctively, shy away from his excessive approaches, fearing the damage he might inflict.

There could now only be compromise, never again the fine intimacy they had known. The awful sadness of it sank heavily further to repress her spirit. What she found so dreadful was the lack of choice. She was committed, maternally, biologically, instinctively, always to the weakest and least defensible.

The atmosphere was shattered as Spud burst in through the doorway shouldering a small paper-wrapped bag of coal. Triumphant in exhaustion he shouted, "I won, it's me the winner!"

"Second!" Hammy acclaimed. They stood, breathing heavily, as if awaiting their deserved applause.

"Get your hands washed the pair of you!" Beenie said brusquely.

They giggled, conspiratorial in their obedience, and went directly to the sink. Too content to have offered objection and invited disruption. Playfully each flicked fingertips of water into the other's eyes.

Beenie's features darkened physically under the strain. She poured the tea and placed out some chocolate biscuits—a full dozen, they vanished almost instantly. Their three brown-rimmed mouths and voraciously munching lips pained her vision—it seemed akin to a physical assault directed explicitly in her direction.

"I've heard o' greed – !" she wailed, agonised that they should inflict this upon her. "But you three!"

Spud, considering it more than his due that in respect to his previous generosity he be allowed to reign supreme for the remainder of the day, pointed a finger so that she might be in no doubt as to whom he was addressing. "Just you keep your mouth shut, that's whit they were there for—eatin'!"

The inevitable hiatus between peace and discord. A mutual dreading of what seemed to be the inevitable. All four paused. Prisoners of all of the previous altercations that served so firmly to predict and direct their responses.

Almost unconsciously Beenie went through the motions of sweeping the floor. When she finally did look up into their expectant faces she said, "I could fairly do wi' a new pair of curtains, them up there are a right mess." Her tone was blank.

In confusion the boys and their father collapsed into a wary silence.

"Mrs White had a fright
In the middle o' the night,
She saw a ghost eatin' toast
Half-way up a lamppost!" Hammy chanted.

Angus, once again bored, wandered by his side around the dullness of the back court.

"Can I go and look in the middens for lucky things?" Angus begged.

"Naw!"

"Aw, how no' . . . ?"

" 'Cause you'll get manky and I'll get belted for it!"

"Can I play wi' your motor now that it's broke?"

"Naw!"

"How no', it's no' worth anything noo?"

"Jist because."

Sunday was a terrible day for them. It lacked the interest of a weekday and the excitement of a Saturday. It was a nothing day.

"Where does the dark go when the sun comes oot, Hammy?"

"Dae you never stop askin' daft questions?" Hammy retorted. "You don't hear big folk askin' questions all the time, dae you?"

"Naw."

"Well then. . . ."

They had been wandering around this tight circle for more than two hours; with each step it seemed to grow oppressively smaller.

"Hallo, hen!" Grinning euphorically, Spud entered the kitchen.

Beenie glanced up with feigned amazement. "They're no' shutting for half an hour yet, whit happened, was there a fire?"

"I've had enough to be goin' on with."

"That's as plain as day."

"Besides," he added, altering his tone to that of muted sex, "I had more important things on my mind when I left."

Stronger again, due to her pills, Beenie replied, "If it's the same things as are glintin' in your eyes then you can forget them!"

"Aw, come on, dae I no' get a wee thank you for the extra two quid?"

"Aye, well, there is that of course," she replied, acknowledging the debt. "See me round about bedtime."

"I'd blow up and burst afore then," he laughed, his confidence growing.

Hammy rushed in through the front door. "Is my Da back frae the pub yet?" he shouted breathlessly. Halting abruptly at the sight of Spud. "Hallo, Da?"

"Away out again, Hammy," Spud pleaded. "Your mother an' me are busy right now!"

Evasively, Beenie turned her attentions towards the boy. "You've no' gone and left that wean oot there by himself?"

"He's aw right," Hammy replied, his voice lacking assurance.

"You've better no' be lying tae me?" she stated fearfully. "The streets these days, if the weans arenae bein' knocked doon they're being abused by some mental pervert!"

"Somebody's watchin' him," Hammy lied.

"Never mind that, Beenie. Send the boy out an' let's you and me talk nice. . . ?"

Unable to deflect herself from the pull of this flattery, Beenie softened. Her dissident body opposed her mind's urge to be desired. "You and your talk," she replied lightly, "jist look where it got me." She looked at him, wanting to see in him a paramour. A hint of promise. A lover. Anything. But he was drunk and she realised that she would be unable to face the sweaty struggle that the reality of it would prove to be.

"I don't remember you complainin' at the time." Spud grinned—a memory of heat.

She nodded, accepting this. "I was three-quarters way full o' vodka and lime and bein' lifted as near as I'll ever get tae heaven on this earth after havin' spent the entire day ower stove and sink. Who's capable o' thought at a time like that. . . ?" She frowned. "Jist once I'd like tae have one that was planned aforehand."

"Da. . . ?" Hammy insisted, reminding them of his presence.

"Will you stop pesterin' me and away oot!" Spud snapped.

Welcoming the intervention Beenie came to her son's aid. "He's been standin' there like a wee martyr, it's only right you should see whit he wants."

Hammy proffered a toy motor car with a twisted wheel. "Can you fix it, I said you could fix it, it's only a wee bit broke?"

Spud glanced at it. "Nae bother, two seconds!" He was genuinely pleased at the apparent brevity of the task. "Now right oot again when it's finished."

"Dead gemmie," Hammy danced. "I told them you could, I told them you could fix anythin'!"

Spud went to his box and unsteadily retrieved his pliers while Beenie, moving adroitly around him, lifted a basin full of wrung-out clothes. "I'll away doon the back and hang these out. I don't suppose any o' you two are goin' to put yourselves out o' joint offerin' to give a hand?" No reply was forthcoming; she had not expected any. Directly to Spud she said, "And jist you mind you don't go and break that thing allthegither, the state you're in!" With that she left.

"You'll no' break it, will you, Da?" Hammy questioned fearfully, having already noted his father's condition.

Spud considered himself above reply. "You brought it tae the right man!" he said, as if to himself, and listening to his own voice reassuringly.

"I told them that!" Hammy informed with pride.

"Aye, who. . . ?"

"Every one o' my pals, especially Tattie!"

"Tattie McFee, Geordie McFee's boy?"

"He's my bestest pal."

Spud looked disgruntled. "Canny say I think aw that much o' his faither—a right big blaw. Good for pushin' people aboot jist because he used tae be a bit o' a boxer!"

"It's Tattie's motor, we swapped."

The wheel refused to straighten, first bending too extreme in one direction and then in the other. "Was it broken when you swapped?"

"Same as now."

"That's my boy," Spud sang gleefully, "sharp as the November wind. Sure I'll fix it for him, why no'? Bet that faither o' his couldnae, big animal that he is." With revitalised enthusiasm he once again bent to the task. "Come on. . . ." He grinned, ceasing momentarily as a further thought struck him. He looked up. "Let's have a gander at whit you wangled out o' him?"

Proudly, and with an adequate amount of flourish, Hammy produced his prize. It was a Joan the Wad charm piece. "I've been tryin' tae get it aff him for ages," he enthused. "It's a magic thing, it works and all, I've seen it, Tattie finds things all the time."

"You've been had!" Spud retorted angrily. "Taken tae the cleaners."

"Naw, Da?" Hammy replied with astonishment.

Spud's features darkened with thought. "Did that yin threaten you and make you swap?"

"He's my bestest pal, Da. He only gave it me because o' that. Everybody's wanted it for ages."

"I'm no' havin' you bein' scared o' him nor naebody else, dae you hear me? I'm no' havin' nae mammy's boy in my family. You should have stood up tae him and fought back like you know I would have done!"

"But I'm a good fighter, Da. I can beat Tattie. . . !"

"Nae need tae make it worse by tellin' lies, I'm no' havin' nae boy o' mine makin' a fool of himself in front o' the entire street." Frustratedly he tugged at the pliers. The plastic shell of the car was already cracking under the strain.

Before such unwarranted suggestions, Hammy experienced a sense of utter bewilderment. Cautious of his father's mounting fury he attempted to further explain. "But it's no' like that . . ."

"Dae you think I don't know these people?" He glared, then, after thinking, dropped his tone to the level of a friendly conspirator. "Look, tell you whit, run doon and give him that stupid thing back. Jist tell him the motor is broken and the deal is off, how's that. . . ?"

Awestruck by such dishonesty Hammy faltered. "We wet thumbs and palmed on it, Da. Nae turn-roons, nae changey-backs. I don't want tae anyway, I've always wanted this thing, it's smashin' so it is!"

"You're scared!" Spud accused. "Yella. I'm no' havin' nae cowards in this family; we might be a lot o' things but we've nane o' us ever been guilty o' that!" Having momentarily forgotten the fragility of the task he compressed the pliers and the toy split from end to end with a loud crack! "Noo look whit you've gone and made me dae!"

"It's broke!"

"Course it's broke, whit else did you expect, pesterin' me while I was workin' on it?"

"You broke it. . . ."

"Never mind," Spud consoled, considering that the matter had now settled itself. "I'll buy you another wan—two if you like. There, how's that— two motors."

"It wasnae mine, it was Tattie's!" Only his astonishment served to restrain his tears.

"Don't you go startin' that again," Spud warned. "The motor is yours, and that daft wee lassie's doll is his! Now forget it, I'm no' askin' any more, I'm tellin' that's an end to it!"

They existed now in a realm previously unknown to them, from lack of experience their emotions floundered hopelessly. Each wishing for some timely intervention which might somehow and miraculously undo all that had gone immediately before. They viewed each other strangely. Sudden strangers and appalled by their own sense of deprivation.

Thankfully, Beenie arrived. Herself an animal raised within a confined and therefore hostile environment, her keen senses caught the situation instantaneously. "You could cut this atmosphere wi' a knife," she commented.

"It's this boy!" Spud volunteered. "I'm right fed up wi' the very sight o' him!"

Beenie directed her eyes towards the ceiling. "Five minutes I've been away." Her gaze lowered and fell upon the broken toy. "You've no' gone and broke the wean's motor?"

"It was Tattie's," Hammy said, allowing his tears to flow.

"He wants tae play wi' dolls noo!"

Habitually, Beenie closed the argument out of her mind. In order to survive she contended only with the untrivial ones. She directed herself to Hammy. "Away doon and fetch the wean up, the dinner's near ready." Hammy shuffled uncomfortably. "Don't jist stand there, go and get him."

"He ran away frae me," Hammy confessed, " 'cause I wouldnae let him play wi' me and my pals."

"He did whit!"

"I tried tae catch him," Hammy explained fearfully, "but he was too fast."

"I'll murder him, the wee bissim!" Beenie exclaimed. "Aw this time, anythin' could be happening tae him, he could be gettin' his throat cut, or even worse." She turned to Spud for comfort but he was, from lack of sustenance, beginning to nod off. "Trust a man," she roared indignantly. "Your youngest could be lyin' in the street wi' nae heid on his shoulders!" She went on a frantic search for her pills. "You, Hammy, you get yourself doon them stairs an' don't you dare show your face through that door again withoot him!" She glanced towards the stove. "If that dinner gets ruined I'll make a hole in the Clyde with the lot of yous!"

The kitchen door burst open.

"I've got him, Ma!" Hammy shouted, dragging a reluctant, kicking Angus in behind him.

"You're nothin' but a big, snottery-nosed sneak!" Angus screamed.

Beenie erupted, unable to restrain herself despite the pills. "Bad wee bugger! Have you any notion o' whit you've been puttin' me through?"

"I was only hiding doon the close," Angus explained, hopeful of avoiding punishment, and now over-eager to converse with her.

"Near aff my heid, I was!" Beenie flyted. Her hand flew out and connected with the side of his face. He went tottering across and then down on to the floor. "Get up!" she demanded, feeling that her rage would only be diminished in the act of knocking him down once again.

"That was sore," Angus pouted.

The childishness of his expression touched her maternal instincts and she limited herself to a further verbal assault. "If your faither wasnae sleepin', I'd batter the living daylights out o' you!"

"Who the hell can sleep wi' this racket goin' on?" Spud asked, disgruntled.

"You!" Beenie turned upon him. "Some faither . . . that wean could have been in hospital fightin' for his very breath and all you can do is sleep!"

Not yet fully released from sleep Spud ignored the challenge. "Whit's that terrible smell?"

"That," Beenie ranted, "is whit's left o' the dinner I spent hours makin'!

You two," she turned upon the children, "get into that room till you're shouted, and you," she turned to Spud, "jist let me hear wan word out o' you aboot your belly rumblin' and I'll stick a knife in it!"

In the face of her awful wrath they obeyed. Deriving energy from her anger Beenie set about preparing yet another meal.

In the darkness of the late-night room Angus lay awakened listening to the voices of his parents in the kitchen. He could see coloured pictures whenever he closed his eyes. Superman in light blue and red, Spiderman casting dark webs. Images from the colour telly. Hammy was awake. Even through the blackness he could sense it.

"Hammy?" he whispered. There was no reply. He tried again. "Hammy. . . ?"

"Whit?"

"Are you wakened?"

"Naw, I'm sleepin', leave me be." There was a certain sadness to his tone.

"Can you no' waken up for a wee minute and talk tae me?"

"Naw!"

The reply was firm.

In the kitchen Beenie hauled herself from her chair and switched off the television before the broadcasting company could coerce her into being assaulted by their nightly rendering of "God Save the Queen".

"Dae they do that on purpose, do you think?"

"Whit?"

"Make the adverts better than the programmes."

Spud, heavy from the want of sleep, did not reply.

"The weans enjoyed the space monster picture earlier on," she continued. "Big saft nellie that you are, buyin' them all o' them sweeties, you near made the two o' them sick."

"Ach, they deserved it, Sunday's a lousy day at the best o' times," he yawned. "Here, whit was the matter wi' oor Hammy?"

"Nothin'," Beenie frowned. "He jist fell aff his rocky-horse for the first time and discovered that the ground is hard."

"Whit rocky-horse. . . ?"

Beenie nodded, unheeding. "Fancy a cup o' tea?"

"Whit I want doesnae come out o' teapots."

"We'll have tea." She filled the kettle.

Angus, having remained silent for as long as possible, whispered, "Hammy?"

"I'm goin' tae throttle you in a minute," Hammy menaced in the dark.

"I want tae ask you somethin'."

"I don't know nothin'!"

"It's jist a wee thing." Angus pleaded. "It's no' even the size o' nothin'."

"Aw right then, whit is it?"

"How's it no' rainin' yet, Hammy. . . ?"

"How should I know?"

"You said it would?"

"Ach, that . . ."

"Did you no' dae it right, is it no' goin' tae rain now?"

"Naw . . . noo get tae sleep."

"But how no', Hammy?"

"Jist because, that's aw. . . ."

They listened, each to the breathing of the other.

"Were you only kidding me?" Angus questioned.

Hammy nodded unseen. "Dae you think I'm simple enough tae believe in daft things the likes o' that? Noo let me get some sleep, I've got school tae go to in the mornin'."

In the pitch they hearkened to breathing and the muted whisperings from through the wall.

"Come on." Spud frowned, afraid of falling asleep before his request had been fulfilled. "Let's get tae bed?"

"Is that all you ever think o'?" Beenie asked, clearing the dishes.

"I've had my drink and I've had my telly, whit else is there?"

She nodded philosophically. "You go on, I'll jist wash through their socks and underpants then I'll be right with you."

"You'll come now, you're no' goin' to be up half the night?"

"I'll be there, jist you go on in and get the bed warm."

Lacking sufficient energy to do otherwise, Spud complied.

Soon he was asleep. Beenie, by the sink, listened to his snores and heard them as the most pleasant sound of her day. With a grunt his body rolled over, his snores subsided, and he dreamed.

She paused,
halting her actions
so that
there might be
Silence. . . .

Smeddum

Lewis Grassic Gibbon

S HE'D had nine of a family in her time, Mistress Menzies, and brought
the nine of them up, forbye—some near by the scruff of the neck, you
would say. They were sniftering and weakly, two-three of the bairns,
sniftering in their cradles to get into their coffins; but she'd shake them to life,
and dose them with salts and feed them up till they couldn't but live. And she'd
plonk one down—finishing the wiping of the creature's neb or the unco
dosing of an ill bit stomach or the binding of a broken head—with a look on
her face as much as to say "Die on me now and see what you'll get!"

Big-boned she was by her fortieth year, like a big roan mare, and "If ever
she was bonny 'twas in Noah's time," Jock Menzies, her eldest son would say.
She'd reddish hair and a high, skeugh nose, and a hand that skelped her way
through life; and if ever a soul had seen her at rest when the dark was done
and the day was come he'd died of the shock and never let on.

For from morn till night she was at it, work, work, on that ill bit croft that
sloped to the sea. When there wasn't a mist on the cold, stone parks there was
more than likely the wheep of the rain, wheeling and dripping in from the sea
that soughed and plashed by the land's stiff edge. Kinneff lay north, and at
night in the south, if the sky was clear on the gloaming's edge, you'd see in
that sky the Bervie lights come suddenly lit, far and away, with the quiet
about you as you stood and looked, nothin to hear but a sea-bird's cry.

But feint the much time to look or to listen had Margaret Menzies of
Tocherty toun. Day blinked and Meg did the same, and was out, up out of her
bed, and about the house, making the porridge and rousting the bairns, and
out to the byre to milk the three kye, the morning growing out in the east and

a wind like a hail of knives from the hills. Syne back to the kitchen again she would be, and catch Jock, her eldest, a clour in the lug that he hadn't roused up his sisters and brothers; and rouse them herself, and feed them and scold, pull up their breeks and straighten their frocks, and polish their shoes and set their caps straight. "Off you get and see you're not late," she would cry, "and see you behave yourselves at the school. And tell the Dominie I'll be down the night to ask him what the mischief he meant by leathering Jeannie and her not well."

They'd cry "Ay, Mother" and go trotting away, a fair flock of the creatures, their faces red-scoured. Her own as red, like a meikle roan mare's, Meg'd turn at the door and go prancing in; and then at last, by the closet-bed, lean over and shake her man half-awake. "Come on, then, Willie, it's time you were up."

And he'd groan and say "Is't?" and crawl out at last, a little bit thing like a weasel, Will Menzies, though some said that weasels were decent beside him. He was drinking himself into the grave, folk said, as coarse a little brute as you'd meet, bone lazy forbye, and as sly as sin. Rampageous and ill with her tongue though she was, you couldn't but pity a woman like Meg tied up for life to a thing like *that*. But she'd more than a soft side still to the creature, she'd half-skelp the backside from any of the bairns she found in the telling of a small bit lie; but when Menzies would come paiching in of a noon and groan that he fair was tashed with his work, he'd mended all the ley fence that day and he doubted he'd need to be off to his bed—when he'd told her that and had ta'en to the blankets, and maybe in less than the space of an hour she'd hold out for the kye and see that he'd lied, the fence neither mended nor letten a be, she'd just purse up her meikle wide mouth and say nothing, her eyes with a glint as though she half-laughed. And when he came drunken home from a mart she'd shoo the children out of the room, and take off his clothes and put him to bed, with an extra nip to keep off a chill.

She did half his work in the Tocherty parks, she'd yoke up the horse and the sholtie together, and kilt up her skirts till you'd see her great legs, and cry "Wissh!" like a man and turn a fair drill, the sea-gulls cawing in a cloud behind, the wind in her hair and the sea beyond. And Menzies with his sly-like eyes would be off on some drunken ploy to Kineff or Stonehive. Man, you couldn't but think as you saw that steer it was well that there was a thing like marriage, folk held together and couldn't get apart; else a black look-out it well would be for the fusionless creature of Tocherty toun.

Well, he drank himself to his grave at last, less smell on the earth if maybe more in it. But she broke down and wept, it was awful to see, Meg Menzies weeping like a stricken horse, her eyes on the dead, quiet face of her man. And she ran from the house, she was gone all that night, though the bairns cried and cried her name up and down the parks in the sound of the sea. But next morning they found her back in their midst, brisk as ever, like a great-boned mare, ordering here and directing there, and a fine feed set the next day for the folk that came to the funeral of her orra man.

She'd four of the bairns at home when he died, the rest were in kitchen-service or fee'd, she'd seen to the settling of the queans herself; and twice when two of them had come home, complaining-like of their mistresses' ways, she'd thrashen the queans and taken them back—near scared the life from the doctor's wife, her that was mistress to young Jean Menzies. "I've skelped the lassie and brought you her back. But don't you ill-use her, or I'll skelp you as well."

There was a fair speak about that at the time, Meg Menzies and the vulgar words she had used, folk told that she'd even said what was the place where she'd skelp the bit doctor's wife. And faith! that fair must have been a sore shock to the doctor's wife that was that genteel she'd never believed she'd a place like that.

Be that as it might, her man new dead, Meg wouldn't hear of leaving the toun. It was harvest then and she drove the reaper up and down the long, clanging clay rigs by the sea, she'd jump down smart at the head of a bout and go gathering and binding swift as the wind, syne wheel in the horse to the cutting again. She led the stooks with her bairns to help, you'd see them at night a drowsing cluster under the moon on the harvesting cart.

And through that year and into the next and so till the speak died down in the Howe Meg Menzies worked the Tocherty toun; and faith, her crops came none so ill. She rode to the mart at Stonehive when she must, on the old box-cart, the old horse in the shafts, the cart behind with a sheep for sale or a birn of old hens that had finished with laying. And a butcher once tried to make a bit joke. "That's a sheep like yourself, fell long in the tooth." And Meg answered up, neighing like a horse, and all heard, "Faith, then, if you've got a spite against teeth I've a clucking hen in the cart outbye. It's as toothless and senseless as you are, near."

The word got about of her eldest son, Jock Menzies that was fee'd up Allardyce way. The creature of a loon had had fair a conceit since he'd won a prize at a ploughing match—not for his ploughing, but for good looks; and the queans about were as daft as himself, he'd only to nod and they came to his heel; and the stories told they came further than that. Well, Meg'd heard the stories and paid no heed, till the last one came, she was fell quick then.

Soon's she heard it she hove out the old bit bike that her daughter Kathie had bought for herself, and got on the thing and went cycling away down through the Bervie braes in that spring, the sun was out and the land lay green with a blink of mist that was blue on the hills, as she came to the toun where Jock was fee'd she saw him out in a park by the road, ploughing, the black loam smooth like a ribbon turning and wheeling at the tail of the plough. Another billy came ploughing behind, Meg Menzies watched till they reached the rig-end, her great chest heaving like a meikle roan's, her eyes on the shape of the furrows they made. And they drew to the end and drew the horse out, and Jock cried "Ay", and she answered back "Ay", and looked at the drill, and gave a bit snort, "If your looks win prizes, your ploughing never will."

Jock laughed, "Fegs, then, I'll not greet for that," and chirked to his horses and turned them about. But she cried him, "Just bide a minute, my lad. What's this I hear about you and Ag Grant?"

He drew up short then, and turned right red, the other childe as well, and they both gave a laugh, as ploughchildes do when you mention a quean they've known overwell in more ways than one. And Meg snapped, "It's an answer I want, not a cockerel's cackle. I can hear that at home on my own dunghill. What are you to do about Ag and her pleiter?"

And Jock said "Nothing", impudent as you like, and next minute Meg was in over the dyke and had hold of his lug and shook him and it till the other childe ran and caught at her nieve. "Faith, mistress, you'll have his lug off!" he cried. But Meg Menzies turned like a mare on new grass, "Keep off or I'll have yours off as well!"

So he kept off and watched, fair a story he'd to tell when he rode out that night to go courting his quean. For Meg held to the lug till it near came off and Jock swore that he'd put things right with Ag Grant. She let go the lug then and looked at him grim, "See that you do and get married right quick, you're the like that needs loaded with a birn of bairns—to keep you out of the jail, I jaloose. It needs smeddum to be either right coarse or right kind."

They were wed before the month was well out, Meg found them a cottar house to settle and gave them a bed and a press she had, and two-three more sticks from Tocherty toun. And she herself led the wedding dance, the minister in her arms, a small bit childe; and 'twas then as she whirled him about the room, he looked like a rat in the teeth of a tyke, that he thanked her for seeing Ag out of her soss, "There's nothing like a marriage for redding things up." And Meg Menzies said "EH?" and then she said "Ay", but queer-like, he supposed she'd no thought of the thing. Syne she slipped off to sprinkle thorns in the bed and to hang below it the great handbell that the bothy-billies took them to every bit marriage.

Well, that was Jock married and at last off her hands. But she'd plenty left still, Dod, Kathleen and Jim that were still at school, Kathie a limmer that alone tongued her mother, Jeannie that next led trouble to her door. She'd been found at her place, the doctor's it was, stealing some money and they sent her home. Syne news of the thing got into Stonehive, the police came out and tormented her sore, she swore she never had stolen a meck, and Meg swore with her, she was black with rage. And folk laughed right hearty, fegs! That was a clour for meikle Meg Menzies, her daughter a thief!

But it didn't last long, it was only three days when folk saw the doctor drive up in his car. And out he jumped and went striding through the close and met face to face with Meg at the door. And he cried "Well, mistress, I've come over for Jeannie." And she glared at him over her high, skeugh nose, "Ay, have you so then? And why, may I speir?"

So he told her why, the money they'd missed had been found at last in a press by the door; somebody or other had left it there, when paying a grocer or such at the door. And Jeannie—he'd come over to take Jean back.

But Meg glared, "Ay, well, you've made another mistake. Out of this, you and your thieving suspicions together!" The doctor turned red. "You're making a miserable error"—and Meg said, "I'll make you mincemeat in a minute."

So he didn't wait that, she didn't watch him go, but went ben to the kitchen where Jeannie was sitting, her face chalk-white as she'd heard them speak. And what happened then a story went round, Jim carried it to school, and it soon spread out, Meg sank in a chair, they thought she was greeting; syne she raised up her head and they saw she was laughing, near as fearsome the one as the other, they thought. "Have you any cigarettes?" she snapped sudden at Jean, and Jean quavered "No," and Meg glowered at her cold. "Don't sit there and lie. Gang bring them to me." And Jean brought them, her mother took the pack in her hand. "Give's hold of a match till I light up the thing. Maybe smoke'll do good for the crow that I got in the throat last night by the doctor's house."

Well, in less than a month she'd got rid of Jean—packed off to Brechin the quean was, and soon got married to a creature there—some clerk that would have left her sore in the lurch but that Meg went down to the place on her bike, and there, so the story went, kicked the childe so that he couldn't sit down for a fortnight, near. No doubt that was just a bit lie that they told, but faith! Meg Menzies had herself to blame, the reputation she'd gotten in the Howe, folk said, "She'll meet with a sore heart yet". But devil a sore was there to be seen, Jeannie was married and was fair genteel.

Kathleen was next to leave home at the term. She was tall, like Meg, and with red hair as well, but a thin fine face, long eyes blue-grey like the hills on a hot day, and a mouth with lips you thought over thick. And she cried, "Ah well, I'm off then, Mother." And Meg cried, "See you behave yourself." And Kathleen cried, "Maybe, I'm not at school now."

Meg stood and stared after the slip of a quean, you'd have thought her half-angry, half near to laughing, as she watched that figure, so slender and trig, with its shoulders square-set slide down the hill on the wheeling bike, swallows were dipping and flying by Kinneff, she looked light and free as a swallow herself, the quean, as she biked away from her home, she turned at the bend and waved and whistled, she whistled like a loon and as loud, did Kath.

Jim was the next to leave from the school, he bided at home and he took no fee, a quiet-like loon, and he worked the toun, and, wonder of wonders, Meg took a rest. Folk said that age was telling a bit on even Meg Menzies at last. The grocer made hints at that one night, and Meg answered up smart as ever of old, "Damn the age! But I've finished the trauchle of the bairns at last, the most of them married or still over young. I'm as swack as ever I was, my lad. But I've just got the notion to be a bit sweir."

Well, she'd hardly begun on that notion when faith! Ill the news that came up to the place from Segget. Kathleen her quean that was fee'd down there, she'd ta'en up with some coarse old childe in a bank, he'd left his wife, they were off together, and she but a bare sixteen years old.

And that proved the truth of what folk were saying, Meg Menzies she hardly paid heed to the news, just gave a bit laugh like a neighing horse and went on with the work of park and byre, cool as you please—ay, getting fell old.

No more was heard of the quean or the man till a two years or more had passed and then word came up to the Tocherty someone had seen her—and where do you think? Out on a boat that was coming from Australia. She was working as stewardess on that bit boat, and the childe that saw her was young John Robb, an emigrant back from his uncle's farm, near starved to death he had been down there. She hadn't met in with him near till the end, the boat close to Southampton the evening they met. And she'd known him at once, though he not her, she'd cried "John Robb?" and he'd answered back "Ay?" and looked at her canny in case it might be the creature was looking for a tip from him. Syne she'd laughed, "Don't you know me, then, you gowk? I'm Kathie Menzies you knew long syne—it was me ran off with the banker from Segget!"

He was clean dumbfounded, young Robb, and he gaped, and then they shook hands and she spoke some more, though she hadn't much time, they were serving up dinner for the first-class folk, aye dirt that are ready to eat and to drink. "If ever you get near to Tocherty toun tell Meg I'll get home and see her some time. Ta-ta!" And then she was off with a smile, young Robb he stood and he stared where she'd been, he thought her the bonniest thing that he'd seen all the weary weeks that he'd been from home.

And this was the tale that he brought to Tocherty, Meg sat and listened and smoked like a tink, forbye herself there was young Jim there, and Jock and his wife and their three bit bairns, he'd fair changed with marriage, had young Jock Menzies. For no sooner had he taken Ag Grant to his bed than he'd started to save, grown mean as dirt, in a three-four years he's finished with feeing, now he rented a fell big farm himself, well stocked it was, and he fee'd two men. Jock himself had grown thin in a way, like his father but worse his bothy childes said, old Menzies at least could take a bit dram and get lost to the world but the son was that mean he might drink rat-poison and take no harm, 'twould feel at home in a stomach like his.

Well, that was Jock, and he sat and heard the story of Kath and her say on the boat. "Ay, still a coarse bitch, I have not a doubt. Well if she never comes back to the Mearns, in Segget you cannot but redden with shame when a body will ask 'Was Kath Menzies your sister?'"

And Ag, she'd grown a great sumph of a woman, she nodded to that, it was only too true, a sore thing it was on decent bit folks that they should have any relations like Kath.

But Meg just sat there and smoked and said never a word, as though she thought nothing worth a yea or a nay. Young Robb had fair ta'en a fancy to Kath and he near boiled up when he heard Jock speak, him and the wife that he'd married from her shame. So he left them short and went raging home, and wished for one that Kath would come back, a summer noon as he cycled home, snipe were calling in the Auchindreich moor where the cattle stood with their tails a-switch, the Grampians rising far and behind, Kinraddie spread like a map for show, its ledges veiled in a mist from the sun. You felt on that day a wild, daft unease, man, beast and bird : as though something were missing and lost from the world, and Kath was the thing that John Robb missed, she'd something in her that minded a man of a house that was builded upon a hill.

Folk thought that maybe the last they would hear of young Kath Menzies and her ill-getted ways. So fair stammy-gastered they were with the news she'd come back to the Mearns, she was down in Stonehive, in a grocer's shop, as calm as could be, selling out tea and cheese and such-like with no blush of shame on her face at all, to decent women that were properly wed and had never looked on men but their own, and only on them with their braces buttoned.

It just showed you the way that the world was going to allow an ill quean like that in a shop, some folk protested to the creature that owned it, but he just shook his head, "Ah well, she works fine; and what else she does is no business of mine." So you well might guess there was more than business between the man and Kath Menzies, like.

And Meg heard the news and went into Stonehive, driving her sholtie, and stopped at the shop. And some in the shop knew who she was and minded the things she had done long syne to other bit bairns of hers that went wrong; and they waited with their breaths held up with delight. But all that Meg did was to nod to Kath, "Ay, well, then, it's you"—"Ay, Mother, just that"— "Two pounds of syrup and see that it's good."

And not another word passed between them, Meg Menzies that once would have ta'en such a quean and skelped her to rights before you could wink. Going home from Stonehive she stopped by the farm where young Robb was fee'd, he was out in the hayfield coiling the hay, and she nodded to him grim, with her high horse face. "What's this that I heard about you and Kath Menzies?"

He turned right red, but he wasn't ashamed. "I've no idea—though I hope it's the worse—It fell near is—Then I wish it was true, she might marry me, then, as I've prigged her to do."

"Oh, have you so, then?" said Meg, and drove home, as though the whole matter was a nothing to her.

But next Tuesday the postman brought a bit note from Kathie. It was to her mother at Tocherty: *Dear Mother, John Robb's going out to Canada and wants me to marry him and go with him. I've told him instead I'll go with him and see what he's like as a man—and then marry him at leisure, if I feel in the mood. But he's hardly any money, and we want to borrow some, so he and I are coming over on Sunday. I hope that you'll have dumpling for tea. Your own daughter, Kath.*

Well, Meg passed that letter over to Jim, he glowered at it dour, "I know— near all the Howe's heard. What are you going to do, now, Mother?"

But Meg just lighted a cigarette and said nothing, she'd smoked like a tink since that steer with Jean. There was promise of strange on-goings at Tocherty by the time that the Sabbath day was come. For Jock came there on a visit as well, him and his wife, and besides him was Jeannie, her that had married the clerk down in Brechin, and she brought the bit creature, he fair was a toff; and he stepped like a cat through the sharn in the close; and when he had heard the story of Kath, her and her plan and John Robb and all, he was shocked near to death, and so was his wife. And Jock Menzies gaped and gave a mean laugh. "Ay, coarse to the bone, ill-getted I'd say if it wasn't that we came of the same bit stock. Ah well, she'll fair have to tramp to Canada, eh Mother?—If she's looking for money from you."

And Meg answered quiet, "No, I wouldn't say that. I've the money all ready for them when they come."

You could hear the sea plashing down soft on the rocks, there was such a dead silence in Tocherty house. And then Jock habbered like a cock with fits: "What, give silver to one who does as she likes, and won't marry as you made the rest of us marry? Give silver to one who's no more than a – "

And he called his sister an ill name enough, and Meg sat and smoked looking over the parks. "Ay, just that. You see, she takes after myself."

And Jeannie squeaked "How?" and Meg answered her quiet: "She's fit to be free and to make her own choice the same as myself and the same kind of choice. There was none of the rest of you fit to do that, you'd to marry or burn, so I married you quick. But Kath and me could afford to find out. It all depends if you've smeddum or not."

She stood up then and put her cigarette out, and looked at the gaping gowks she had mothered. "I never married your father, you see. I could never make up my mind about Will. But maybe our Kath will find something surer . . . Here's her and her man coming up the road."

Rab and His Friends

Dr John Brown

F OUR-AND-THIRTY years ago, Bob Ainslie and I were coming up Infirmary
Street from the High School, our heads together, and our arms inter-
twisted, as only lovers and boys know how, or why.

When we got to the top of the street, and turned north, we espied a crowd
at the Tron Church. "A dog-fight!" shouted Bob, and was off; and so was I,
both of us all but praying that it might not be over before we got up! And is
not this boy-nature? And human nature too? And don't we all wish a house
on fire not to be out before we see it? Dogs like fighting; old Isaac says they
"delight" in it, and for the best of all reasons; and boys are not cruel because
they like to see the fight. They see three of the great cardinal virtues of dog or
man—courage, endurance, and skill—in intense action. This is very different
from a love of making dogs fight, and enjoying, and aggravating, and making
gain by their pluck. A boy—be he ever so fond himself of fighting—if he be a
good boy, hates and despises all this, but he would have run off with Bob and
me fast enough: it is a natural, and a not wicked interest, that all boys and
men have in witnessing intense energy in action.

Does any curious and finely-ignorant woman wish to know how Bob's
eye at a glance announced a dog-fight to his brain? He did not, he could not
see the dogs fighting; it was a flash of an inference, a rapid induction. The
crowd round a couple of dogs fighting is a crowd masculine mainly, with an
occasional active, compassionate woman, fluttering wildly round the outside,
and using her tongue and her hands freely upon the men, as so many "brutes";
it is a crowd annular, compact, and mobile; a crowd centripetal, having its
eyes and its heads all bent downwards and inwards to one common focus.

52

Well, Bob and I are up, and find it is not over: a small thoroughbred white bull-terrier is busy throttling a large shepherd's dog, unaccustomed to war, but not to be trifled with. They are hard at it; the scientific little fellow doing his work in great style, his pastoral enemy fighting wildly, but with the sharpest of teeth and a great courage. Science and breeding, however, soon had their own; the Game Chicken, as the premature Bob called him, working his way up, took his final grip of poor Yarrow's throat—and he lay gasping and done for. His master, a brown, handsome, big young shepherd from Tweedsmuir, would have liked to have knocked down any man, would "drink up Esil, or eat a crocodile," for that part, if he had a chance: it was no use kicking the little dog; that would only make him hold the closer. Many were the means shouted out in mouthfuls, of the best possible ways of ending it. "Water!" but there was none near, and many cried for it who might have got it from the well at Blackfriars Wynd. "Bite the tail!" and a large, vague, benevolent, middle-aged man, more desirous than wise, with some struggle got the bushy end of Yarrow's tail into his ample mouth, and bit it with all his might. This was more than enough for the much-enduring, much-perspiring shepherd, who, with a gleam of joy over his broad visage, delivered a terrific facer upon our large, vague, benevolent, middle-aged friend—who went down like a shot.

Still the Chicken holds; death not far off. "Snuff! A pinch of snuff!" observed a calm, highly-dressed young buck, with an eyeglass in his eye. "Snuff, indeed!" growled the angry crowd, affronted and glaring. "Snuff! a pinch of snuff!" again observes the buck, but with more urgency; whereon were produced several open boxes, and from a mull which may have been at Culloden, he took a pinch, knelt down, and presented it to the nose of the Chicken. The laws of physiology and of snuff take their course; the Chicken sneezes, and Yarrow is free!

The young pastoral giant stalks off with Yarrow in his arms—comforting him.

But the bull-terrier's blood is up, and his soul unsatisfied; he grips the first dog he meets, and discovering she is not a dog, in Homeric phrase, he makes a brief sort of *amende,* and is off. The boys, with Bob and me at their head, are after him: down Niddry Street he goes, bent on mischief; up the Cowgate like an arrow—Bob and I, and our small men, panting behind.

There, under the single arch of the South Bridge, is a huge mastiff, sauntering down the middle of the causeway, as if with his hands in his pockets: he is old, grey, brindled, as big as a little Highland bull, and has the Shakespearian dewlaps shaking as he goes.

The Chicken makes straight at him, and fastens on his throat. To our astonishment, the great creature does nothing but stand still, hold himself up, and roar—yes, roar; a long, serious, remonstrative roar. How is this? Bob and I are up to them. *He is muzzled!* The bailies had proclaimed a general muzzling, and his master, studying strength and economy mainly, had encompassed his huge jaws in a home-made apparatus, constructed out of the leather of some ancient breechin'. His mouth was open as far as it could; his lips curled up in rage—a sort of terrible grin; his teeth gleaming ready, from out the darkness; the strap across his mouth tense as a bowstring; his whole frame stiff with indignation and surprise; his roar asking us all round, "Did you ever see the like of this?" He looked a statue of anger and astonishment, done in Aberdeen granite.

We soon had a crowd: the Chicken held on. "A knife!" cried Bob; and a cobbler gave him his knife: you know the kind of knife, worn away obliquely to a point, and always keen. I put its edge to the tense leather; it ran before it; and then!—one sudden jerk of that enormous head, a sort of dirty mist about his mouth, no noise—and the bright and fierce little fellow is dropped, limp, and dead. A solemn pause; this was more than any of us had bargained for. I turned the little fellow over, and saw he was quite dead; the mastiff had taken him by the small of the back like a rat, and broken it.

He looked down at his victim appeased, ashamed, and amazed: snuffed him all over, stared at him, and taking a sudden thought, turned round and trotted off. Bob took the dead dog up, and said, "John, we'll bury him after tea." "Yes," said I, and was off after the mastiff. He made up the Cowgate at a rapid swing; he had forgotten some engagement. He turned up the Candlemaker Row, and stopped at the Harrow Inn.

There was a carrier's cart ready to start, and a keen, thin, impatient, black-a-vised little man, his hand at his grey horse's head, looking about angrily for something. "Rab, ye thief!" said he, aiming a kick at my great friend, who drew cringing up, and avoiding the heavy shoe with more agility than dignity, and watching his master's eye, slunk dismayed under the cart— his eyes down, and as much as he had of tail down too.

What a man this must be—thought I—to whom my tremendous hero turns tail! The carrier saw the muzzle hanging, cut and useless, from his neck, and I eagerly told him the story, which Bob and I always thought and still think, Homer, or King David, or Sir Walter, alone were worthy to rehearse. The severe little man was mitigated, and condescended to say, "Rab, ma man, puir Rabbie,"—whereupon the stump of a tail rose up, the ears were cocked, the eyes filled, and were comforted; the two friends were reconciled. "Hupp!" and a stroke of the whip was given to Jess; and off went the three.

Bob and I buried the Game Chicken that night (we had not much of a tea) in the back-green of his house, in Melville Street, No. 17, with considerable gravity and silence; and being at the time in the *Iliad*, and, like all boys, Trojans, we called him Hector, of course.

Six years have passed—a long time, for a boy and a dog: Bob Ainslie is off to the wars; I am a medical student, and clerk at Minto House Hospital.

Rab I saw almost every week, on the Wednesday, and we had much pleasant intimacy. I found the way to his heart by frequent scratching of his huge head, and an occasional bone. When I did not notice him he would plant himself straight before me, and stand wagging that bud of a tail, and looking up, with his head a little to the one side. His master I occasionally saw; he used to call me "Maister John", but was laconic as any Spartan.

One fine October afternoon, I was leaving the hospital, when I saw the large gate open, and in walked Rab, with that great and easy saunter of his. He looked as if taking general possession of the place; like the Duke of Wellington entering a subdued city, satiated with victory and peace. After him came Jess, now white from age, with her cart; and in it a woman, carefully wrapped up—the carrier leading the horse anxiously, and looking back. When he saw me, James (for his name was James Noble) made a curt and grotesque "boo", and said, "Maister John, this is the mistress. She's got a trouble in her breest—some kind o' an income we're thinkin'."

By this time I saw the woman's face; she was sitting on a sack filled with straw, her husband's plaid round her, and his big coat, with its large white metal buttons, over her feet.

I never saw a more unforgettable face—pale, serious, lonely,* delicate, sweet, without being at all what we call fine. She looked sixty, and had on a mutch, white as snow, with its black ribbon; her silvery, smooth hair setting off her dark grey eyes—eyes such as one sees only twice or thrice in a lifetime, full of suffering, full also of the overcoming of it: her eyebrows black and delicate, and her mouth firm, patient, and contented, which few mouths ever are.

As I have said, I never saw a more beautiful countenance, or one more subdued to settled quiet. "Ailie," said James, "this is Maister John, the young doctor; Rab's freend, ye ken. We often speak aboot you, doctor." She smiled, and made a movement, but said nothing; and prepared to come down, putting her plaid aside and rising. Had Solomon, in all his glory, been handing down the Queen of Sheba at his palace gate, he could not have done it more daintily, more tenderly, more like a gentleman, than did James the Howgate carrier, when he lifted down Ailie his wife. The contrast of his small, swarthy, weather-beaten, keen, worldly face to hers—pale, subdued, and beautiful— was something wonderful. Rab looked on concerned and puzzled, but ready for anything that might turn up—were it to strangle the nurse, the porter, or even me. Ailie and he seemed great friends.

"As I was sayin', she's got a kind o' trouble in her breest, doctor. Wull ye tak' a look at it?" We walked into the consulting room all four; Rab grim and comic, willing to be happy and confidential if cause could be shown, willing also to be the reverse, on the same terms. Ailie sat down, undid her open gown and her lawn handkerchief round her neck, and, without a word, showed me her right breast. I looked at and examined it carefully—she and James watching me, and Rab eyeing all three. What could I say? There it was, that had once been so soft, so shapely, so white, so gracious and bountiful, so "full of all blessed conditions", hard as a stone, a centre of horrid pain,

*It is not easy giving this look by one word; it was expressive of her being so much of her life alone.

making that pale face, with its grey, lucid reasonable eyes, and its sweet resolved mouth, express the full measures of suffering overcome. Why was that gentle, modest sweet woman, clean and lovable, condemned by God to bear such a burden?

I got her away to bed. "May Rab and me bide?" said James. "*You* may; and Rab, if he will behave himself." "I'se warrant he's do that, doctor", and in slunk the faithful beast. I wish you could have seen him. There are no such dogs now. He belonged to a lost tribe. As I have said, he was brindled, and grey like Rubislaw granite; his hair short, hard, and close, like a lion's; his body thickset, like a little bull—a sort of compressed Hercules of a dog. He must have been ninety pounds weight, at the least; he had a large blunt head; his muzzle black as night, his mouth blacker than any night, a tooth or two—being all he had—gleaming out of his jaws of darkness. His head was scarred with the records of old wounds, a sort of series of fields of battle all over it; one eye out, one ear cropped as close as was Archbishop Leighton's father's; the remaining eye had the power of two; and above it, and in constant communication with it, was a tattered rag of an ear, which was for ever unfurling itself, like an old flag; and then that bud of a tail, about one inch long, if it could in any sense be said to be long, being as broad as long—the mobility, the instantaneousness of that bud were very funny and surprising, and its expressive twinklings and winkings, the intercommunications between the eye, the ear and it, were of the oddest and swiftest.

Rab had the dignity and simplicity of great size; and having fought his way all along the road to absolute supremacy, he was as mighty in his own line as Julius Caesar or the Duke of Wellington, and had the gravity of all great fighters.

You must have often observed the likeness of certain men to certain animals, and of certain dogs to men. Now I never looked at Rab without thinking of the great Baptist preacher, Andrew Fuller. The same large, heavy, menacing, combative, sombre, honest countenance, the same deep inevitable eye, the same look—as of thunder asleep, but ready—neither a dog nor a man to be trifled with.

Next day, my master, the surgeon, examined Ailie. There was no doubt it must kill her, and soon. It could be removed—it might never return—it would give her speedy relief—she should have it done. She curtsied, looked at James, and said, "When?" "Tomorrow," said the kind surgeon—a man of few words. She and James and Rab and I retired. I noticed that he and she spoke little, but seemed to anticipate everything in each other. The following day, at noon, the students came in, hurrying up the great stair. At the first landing-place, on a small well-known blackboard, was a bit of paper fastened by wafers, and many remains of old wafers beside it. On the paper were the words: *An operation today. J. B., Clerk.*

Up ran the youths, eager to secure good places: in they crowded, full of interest and talk. "What's the case?" "Which side is it?"

Don't think them heartless; they are neither better nor worse than you or

I: they get over their professional horrors, and into their proper work; and in them pity—as an *emotion*, ending in itself or at best in tears and a long-drawn breath, lessens, while pity as a motive, is quickened and gains power and purpose. It is well for poor human nature that it is so.

The operating theatre is crowded; much talk and fun, and all the cordiality and stir of youth. The surgeon with his staff of assistants is there. In comes Ailie: one look at her quiets and abates the eager students. That beautiful old woman is too much for them; they sit down, and are dumb, and gaze at her. These rough boys feel the power of her presence. She walks in quickly, but without haste; dressed in her mutch, her neckerchief, her white dimity shortgown, her black bombazeen petticoat, showing her white worsted stockings and her carpet-shoes. Behind her was James with Rab. James sat down in the distance, and took that huge and noble head between his knees. Rab looked perplexed and dangerous; forever cocking his ear and dropping it as fast.

Ailie stepped up on a seat, and laid herself on the table, as her friend the surgeon told her; arranged herself, gave a rapid look at James, shut her eyes, rested herself on me, and took my hand. The operation was at once begun; it was necessarily slow; and chloroform—one of God's best gifts to His suffering children—was then unknown. The surgeon did his work. The pale face showed its pain, but was still and silent. Rab's soul was working within him; he saw that something strange was going on—blood flowing from his mistress, and she suffering; his ragged ear was up, and importunate; he growled and gave now and then a sharp impatient yelp; he would have liked to have done something to that man. But James had him firm, and gave him a glower from time to time; and an intimation of a possible kick—all the better for James, it kept his eye and his mind off Ailie.

It is over: she is dressed, steps gently and decently down from the table, looks for James; then, turning to the surgeon and the students, she curtsies—and in a low, clear voice, begs their pardon if she has behaved ill. The students —all of us—wept like children; the surgeon happed her up carefully—and, resting on James and me, Ailie went to her room, Rab following. We put her to bed. James took off his heavy shoes, crammed with tackets, heel-capt, and toe-capt, and put them carefully under the table, saying, "Maister John, I'm for nane o' yer strynge nurse bodies for Ailie. I'll be her nurse, and I'll gang aboot on my stockin' soles as canny as pussy." And so he did; and handy and clever, and swift and tender as any woman, was that horny-handed, snell, peremptory little man. Everything she got he gave her: he seldom slept, and often I saw his small shrewd eyes out of the darkness, fixed on her. As before, they spoke little.

Rab behaved well, never moving, showing us how meek and gentle he could be, and occasionally, in his sleep, letting us know that he was demolishing some adversary. He took a walk with me every day, generally to the Candlemaker Row; but he was sombre and mild; declined doing battle, though some fit cases offered, and indeed submitted to sundry indignities;

and was always very ready to turn, and came faster back, and trotted up the stair with much lightness, and went straight to that door.

Jess, the mare, had been sent, with her weather-worn cart, to Howgate, and had doubtless her own dim and placid meditations and confusions, on the absence of her master and Rab, and her unnatural freedom from the road and her cart.

For some days Ailie did well. The wound healed "by the first intention"; for as James said, "Oor Ailie's skin's ower clean to beil." The students came in quiet and anxious, and surrounded her bed. She said she liked to see their young, honest faces. The surgeon dressed her, and spoke to her in his own short kind way, pitying her through his eyes, Rab and James outside the circle—Rab being now reconciled, and even cordial, and having made up his mind that as yet nobody required worrying, but, as you may suppose, *semper paratus.*

So far well: but, four days after the operation, my patient had a sudden and long shivering, a "groosin'", as she called it. I saw her soon after; her eyes were too bright, her cheek coloured: she was restless, and ashamed of being so; the balance was lost; mischief had begun. On looking at the wound, a blush of red told the secret: her pulse was rapid, her breathing anxious and quick, she wasn't herself, as she said, and was vexed at her restlessness. We tried what we could. James did everything, was everything; never in the way, never out of it; Rab subsided under the table into a dark place, and was motionless, all but his eye, which followed everyone. Ailie got worse; began to wander in her mind, gently; was more demonstrative in her ways to James, rapid in her questions, and sharp at times. He was vexed, and said, "She was never that way afore; no, never." For a time she knew her head was wrong, and was always asking our pardon—the dear, gentle old woman: then delirium set in strong, without pause. Her brain gave way, and then came that terrible spectacle—

> The intellectual power, through words and things,
> Went sounding on its dim and perilous way;

she sang bits of old songs and psalms, stopping suddenly, mingling the Psalms of David, and the diviner words of his Son and Lord, with homely odds and ends and scraps of ballads.

Nothing more touching, or in a sense more strangely beautiful, did I ever witness. Her tremulous, rapid, affectionate, eager Scotch voice—the swift, aimless, bewildered mind, the baffled utterance, the bright and perilous eye; some wild words, some household cares, something for James, the names of the dead, Rab called rapidly and in a "fremyt" voice, and he starting up, surprised, and slinking off as if he were to blame somehow, or had been dreaming he heard. Many eager questions and beseechings which James and I could make nothing of, and on which she seemed to set her all, and then sink back ununderstood. It was very sad, but better than many things that are not called sad. James hovered about, put out and miserable, but active and exact as ever; read to her, when there was a lull, short bits from the Psalms, prose and metre, chanting the latter in his own rude and serious way, showing great knowledge of the fit words, bearing up like a man, and doating over her as his "ain Ailie". "Ailie, ma woman!" "Ma ain bonnie wee dawtie!"

The end was drawing on: the golden bowl was breaking; the silver cord was fast being loosed—that *animula blandula, vagula, hospes, comesque,* was about to flee. The body and soul—companions for sixty years—were being sundered, and taking leave. She was walking alone, through the valley of that shadow, into which one day we must all enter—and yet she was not alone, for we know whose rod and staff were comforting her.

One night she had fallen quiet, and as we hoped, asleep; her eyes were shut. We put down the gas, and sat watching her. Suddenly she sat up in bed, and taking a bed-gown which was lying on it rolled up, she held it eagerly to her breast—to the right side. We could see her eyes bright with a surprising tenderness and joy, bending over this bundle of clothes. She held it as a woman holds her sucking child; opening out her night-gown impatiently, and holding it close, and brooding over it, and murmuring foolish little words, as over one whom his mother comforteth, and who sucks and is satisfied. It was pitiful and strange to see her wasted dying look, keen and yet vague—her immense love.

"Preserve me!" groaned James, giving way. And then she rocked back and forward, as if to make it sleep, hushing it, and wasting on it her infinite fondness. "Wae's me, doctor; I declare she's thinkin' it's that bairn." "What bairn?" "The only bairn we ever had; our wee Mysie, and she's in the Kingdom, forty years and mair." It was plainly true: the pain in the breast, telling its urgent story to a bewildered, ruined brain, was misread and mistaken; it suggested to her the uneasiness of a breast full of milk and then the child; and so again once more they were together, and she had her ain wee Mysie in her bosom.

This was the close. She sank rapidly: the delirium left her; but, as she whispered, she was "clean silly"; it was the lightening before the final darkness. After having for some time lain still—her eyes shut, she said "James!" He came close to her, and lifting up her calm, clear, beautiful eyes, she gave him a long look, turned to me kindly but shortly, looked for Rab but could not see him, then turned to her husband again, as if she would never leave off looking, shut her eyes, and composed herself. She lay for some time breathing quick, and passed away so gently, that when we thought she was gone, James, in his old-fashioned way, held the mirror to her face. After a long pause, one small spot of dimness was breathed out; it vanished away, and never returned, leaving the blank clear darkness of the mirror without a stain. "What is our life? It is even a vapour, which appeareth for a little time, and then vanisheth away."

Rab all this time had been full awake and motionless: he came forward beside us; Ailie's hand, which James had held, was hanging down; it was soaked with his tears; Rab licked it all over carefully, looked at her, and returned to his place under the table.

James and I sat, I don't know how long, but for some time—saying nothing: he started up abruptly, and with some noise went to the table, and putting his right fore and middle finger each into a shoe, pulled them out, and put them on, breaking one of the leather latchets, and muttering in anger, "I never did the like o' that afore!"

I believe he never did; nor after either. "Rab!" he said roughly, and pointing with his thumb to the bottom of the bed. Rab leapt up, and settled himself; his head and eye to the dead face. "Maister John, ye'll wait for me," said the carrier; and disappeared in the darkness, thundering downstairs in his heavy shoes. I ran to a front window: there he was, already round the house, and out at the gate, fleeing like a shadow.

I was afraid about him, and yet not afraid; so I sat down beside Rab, and being wearied, fell asleep. I awoke from a sudden noise outside. It was November, and there had been a heavy fall of snow. Rab was *in statu quo*; he heard the noise too, and plainly knew it, but never moved. I looked out; and there, at the gate, in the dim morning—for the sun was not up, was Jess and the cart—a cloud of steam rising from the old mare. I did not see James; he was already at the door, and came up the stairs, and met me. It was less than three hours since he left, and he must have posted out—who knows how?— to Howgate, full nine miles off; yoked Jess, and driven her astonished into town. He had an armful of blankets, and was streaming with perspiration. He nodded to me, spread out on the floor two pairs of clean old blankets having at their corners, "A. G., 1796," in large letters in red worsted. These were the initials of Alison Graeme, and James may have looked in at her from without—himself unseen but not·unthought of—when he was "wat, wat, and weary," and after having walked many a mile over the hills, may have seen her sitting, while "a' the lave were sleepin'" and by the firelight working her name on the blankets, for her ain James's bed.

He motioned Rab down, and taking his wife in his arms, laid her in the blankets, and happed her carefully and firmly up, leaving the face uncovered; and then lifting her, he nodded again sharply to me, and with a resolved but utterly miserable face, strode along the passage, and downstairs, followed by Rab. I followed with a light; but he didn't need it. I went out, holding stupidly the candle in my hand in the calm frosty air; we were soon at the gate. I could have helped him, but I saw he was not to be meddled with, and he was strong, and did not need it. He laid her down as tenderly, as safely, as he had lifted her out ten days before—as tenderly as when he had her first in his arms when she was only "A. G."—sorted her, leaving that beautiful sealed face open to the heavens; and then taking Jess by the head, he moved away. He did not notice me, neither did Rab, who presided behind the cart.

I stood till they passed through the long shadow of the College, and turned up Nicolson Street. I heard the solitary cart sound through the streets and die away and come again; and I returned, thinking of that company going up

Liberton Brae, then along Roslin Muir, the morning light touching the Pentlands and making them like onlooking ghosts; then down the hill through Auchindinny woods, past "haunted Woodhouselee"; and as daybreak came sweeping up the bleak Lammermuirs, and fell on his own door, the company would stop, and James would take the key and lift Ailie up again, laying her on her own bed, and, having put Jess up, would return with Rab and shut the door.

James buried his wife, with his neighbours mourning, Rab inspecting the solemnity from a distance. It was snow, and that black ragged hole would look strange in the midst of the swelling spotless cushion of white. James looked after everything; then rather suddenly fell ill and took to bed; was insensible when the doctor came, and soon died. A sort of low fever was prevailing in the village, and his want of sleep, his exhaustion, and his misery, made him apt to take it. The grave was not difficult to reopen. A fresh fall of snow had again made all things white and smooth; Rab once more looked on, and slunk home to the stable.

And what of Rab? I asked for him next week at the new carrier who got the goodwill of James's business, and was now master of Jess and her cart. "How's Rab?" He put me off, and said rather rudely, "What's *your* business wi' the dowg?" I was not to be so put off. "Where's Rab?" He, getting confused and red, and intermeddling with his hair, said, "'Deed, sir, Rab's deed" "Dead! What did he die off?" "Weel, sir," said he, getting redder, "he didna exactly dee; he was killed. I had to brain him wi' a rack-pin; there was nae doin' wi' him. He lay in the treviss wi' the mear, and wadna come oot. I tempit him wi' kail and meat, but he wad tak naething, and keepit me frae feedin' the beast, and he was aye gur gurrin', and grup gruppin' me by the legs. I was laith to make awa wi' the auld dowg, his like wasna atween this and Thornhill—but, 'deed, sir, I could dae naething else." I believed him. Fit end for Rab, quick and complete. His teeth and his friends gone, why should he keep the peace and be civil?

He was buried in the braeface, near the burn, the children of the village, his companions, who used to make very free with him and sit on his ample stomach, as he lay half asleep at the door in the sun—watching the solemnity.

Thrawn Janet

R. L. Stevenson

THE Reverend Murdoch Soulis was long minister of the moorland parish of Balweary, in the vale of Dule. A severe, bleak-faced old man, dreadful to his hearers, he dwelt in the last years of his life, without relative or servant or any human company, in the small and lonely manse under the Hanging Shaw. In spite of the iron composure of his features, his eye was wild, scared, and uncertain; and when he dwelt, in private admonitions, on the future of the impenitent, it seemed as if his eye pierced through the storms of time to the terrors of eternity. Many young persons, coming to prepare themselves against the season of the Holy Communion, were dreadfully affected by his talk. He had a sermon on I Peter 5, verse 8, "The devil as a roaring lion", on the Sunday after every seventeenth of August, and he was accustomed to surpass himself upon that text both by the appalling nature of the matter and the terror of his bearing in the pulpit. The children were frightened into fits, and the old looked more than usually oracular, and were, all that day, full of those hints that Hamlet deprecated. The manse itself, where it stood by the water of Dule among some thick trees, with the Shaw overhanging it on the one side, and on the other many cold, moorish hilltops rising towards the sky, had begun, at a very early period of Mr Soulis's ministry, to be avoided in the dusk hours by all who valued themselves upon their prudence; and guidmen sitting at the clachan alehouse shook their heads together at the thought of passing late by the uncanny neighbourhood. There was one spot, to be more particular, which was regarded with especial awe. The manse stood between the high-road and the water of Dule, with a gable to each; its back was towards the kirk-town of Balweary, nearly half a mile away; in front of it, a bare garden, hedged with thorn, occupied the land between the river and the road. The house was two storeys high, with two large rooms on each. It opened not directly on the garden, but on a causewayed path, or passage, giving on the road on the one hand, and closed on the other by the tall willows and elders that bordered on the stream. And it was this strip of causeway that enjoyed among the young parishioners of Balweary so infamous a reputation. The minister walked there often after dark, sometimes groaning aloud in the instancy of his unspoken prayers; and when he was from home, and the manse door was locked, the more daring schoolboys ventured, with beating hearts, to "follow my leader" across that legendary spot.

This atmosphere of terror, surrounding, as it did, a man of God of spotless character and orthodoxy, was a common cause of wonder and subject of inquiry among the few strangers who were led by chance or business into that unknown, outlying country. But many even of the people of the parish were ignorant of the strange events which had marked the first year of Mr Soulis's ministrations; and among those who were better informed, some were naturally reticent, and others shy of that particular topic. Now and again, only, one of the older folk would warm into courage over his third tumbler, and recount the cause of the minister's strange looks and solitary life.

Fifty years syne, when Mr Soulis cam' first into Ba'weary, he was still a young man—a callant, the folk said—fu' o' book learnin' and grand at the exposition, but, as was natural in sae young a man, wi' nae leevin' experience in religion. The younger sort were greatly taken wi' his gifts and his gab; but auld, concerned, serious men and women were moved even to prayer for the young man, whom they took to be a self-deceiver, and the parish that was like to be sae ill-supplied. It was before the days o' the Moderates—weary fa' them; but ill things are like guid—they baith come bit by bit, a pickle at a time; and there were folk even then that said the Lord had left the college professors to their ain devices, an' the lads that went to study wi' them wad hae done mair and better sittin' in a peatbog, like their forebears of the persecution, wi' a Bible under their oxter and a speerit o' prayer in their heart. There was nae doubt, onyway, but that Mr Soulis had been ower lang at the college. He was careful and troubled for mony things besides the ae thing needful. He had a feck o' books wi' him—mair than had ever been seen before in a' that presbytery; and a sair wark the carrier had wi' them, for they were a' like to have smoored in the Deil's Hag between this and Kilmackerlie. They were books o' divinity, to be sure, or so they ca'd them; but the serious were o' opinion there was little service for sae mony, when the hail o' God's Word would gang in the neuk of a plaid. Then he wad sit half the day and half the nicht forbye, which was scant decent—writin' nae less; and first, they were feared he wad read his sermons; and syne it proved he was writin' a book himsel', which was surely no fittin' for ane of his years an' sma' experience.

Onyway it behoved him to get an auld, decent wife to keep the manse for him an' see to his bit denners; and he was recommended to an auld limmer— Janet M'Clour, they ca'd her—and sae far left to himsel' as to be ower persuaded. There was mony advised him to the contrar, for Janet was mair than suspeckit by the best folk in Ba'weary. Lang or that, she had had a wean to a dragoon; she hadnae come forrit* for maybe thretty year; and bairns had seen her mumblin' to hersel' up on Key's Loan in the gloamin', whilk was an unco time an' place for a God-fearin' woman. Howsoever, it was the laird himsel' that had first tauld the minister o' Janet; and in thae days he wad have gane a far gate to pleesure the laird. When folk tauld him that Janet was sib to the deil, it was a' superstition by his way of it; an' when they cast up the Bible to him an' the witch of Endor, he wad threep it doun their thrapples that thir days were a' gane by, and the deil was mercifully restrained.

Weel, when it got about the clachan that Janet M'Clour was to be servant at the manse, the folk were fair mad wi' her an' him thegether; and some o' the guidwives had nae better to dae than get round her door-cheeks and chairge her wi' a' that was ken't again her, frae the sodger's bairn to John Tamson's twa kye. She was nae great speaker; folk usually let her gang her ain gate, an' she let them gang theirs, wi' neither Fair-guid-een nor Fair-guid-day; but when she buckled to, she had a tongue to deave the miller. Up she got, an' there wasnae an auld story in Ba'weary but she gart somebody lowp for it that day; they couldnae say ae thing but she could say twa to it; till, at the hinder end, the guidwives up and claught haud of her, and clawed the coats aff her back, and pu'd her doun the clachan to the water o' Dule, to see if she were a witch or no, soum or droun. The carline skirled till ye could hear her at the Hangin' Shaw, and she focht like ten; there was mony a guidwife bure the mark of her neist day an' mony a lang day after; and just in the hettest o' the collie-shangie, wha suld come up (for his sins) but the new minister.

"Women," said he (and he had a grand voice), "I charge you in the Lord's name to let her go."

Janet ran to him—she was fair wud wi' terror—an' clang to him, an' prayed him, for Christ's sake, save her frae the cummers; an' they, for their pairt, tauld him a' that was ken't, and maybe mair.

"Woman," says he to Janet, "is this true?"

"As the Lord sees me," says she, "as the Lord made me, no a word o't. Forbye the bairn," says she, "I've been a decent woman a' my days."

"Will you," says Mr Soulis, "in the name of God, and before me, His unworthy minister, renounce the devil and his works?"

Weel, it wad appear that when he askit that, she gave a girn that fairly frichit them that saw her, an' they could hear her teeth play dirl thegether in her chafts; but there was naething for it but the ae way or the ither; an' Janet lifted up her hand and renounced the deil before them a'.

"And now," says Mr Soulis to the guidwives, "home with ye, one and all, and pray to God for His forgiveness."

* To come forrit—to offer oneself as a communicant.

And he gied Janet his arm, though she had little on her but a sark, and took her up the clachan to her ain door like a leddy of the land; an' her scrieghin' and laughin' as was a scandal to be heard.

There were mony grave folk lang ower their prayers that nicht; but when the morn cam' there was sic a fear fell upon a' Ba'weary that the bairns hid theirsels, and even the menfolk stood and keekit frae their doors. For there was Janet comin' doun the clachan—her or her likeness, nane could tell—wi' her neck thrawn, and her heid on ae side, like a body that has been hangit, and a girn on her face like an unstreakit corp. By-an'-by they got used wi' it, and even speered at her to ken what was wrang; but frae that day forth she couldnae speak like a Christian woman, but slavered and played click wi' her teeth like a pair o' shears; and frae that day forth the name o' God cam' never on her lips. Whiles she would try to say it, but it michtnae be. Them that kenned best said least; but they never gied that Thing the name o' Janet M'Clour; for the auld Janet, by their way o't, was in muckle hell that day. But the minister was neither to haud nor to bind; he preached about naething but the folk's cruelty that had gi'en her a stroke of the palsy; he skelpt the bairns that meddled her; and he had her up to the manse that same nicht, and dwalled there a' his lane wi' her under the Hangin' Shaw.

Weel, time gaed by: and the idler sort commenced to think mair lichtly o' that black business. The minister was weel thocht o'; he was aye late at the writing, folk wad see his can'le doon by the Dule water after twal' at e'en; and he seemed pleased wi' himsel' and upsitten as at first, though a'body could see that he was dwining. As for Janet she cam' an' she gaed; if she didnae speak muckle afore, it was reason she should speak less then; she meddled naebody; but she was an eldritch thing to see, an' nane wad hae mistrysted wi' her for Ba'weary glebe.

About the end o' July there cam' a spell o' weather, the like o't never was in that countryside; it was lown an' het an' heartless; the herds couldnae win up the Black Hill, the bairns were ower weariet to play; an' yet it was gousty too, wi' claps o' het wund that rumm'led in the glens, and bits o' shouers that slockened naething. We aye thocht it but to thun'er on the morn; but the morn cam', an' the morn's morning, and it was aye the same uncanny weather, sair on folks and bestial. Of a' that were the waur, nane suffered like Mr Soulis; he could neither sleep nor eat, he tauld his elders; an' when he wasnae writin' at his weary book, he wad be stravaguin' ower a' the countryside like a man possessed, when a'body else was blythe to keep caller ben the house.

Abune Hangin' Shaw, in the bield o' the Black Hill, there's a bit enclosed grund wi' an iron yett; and it seems, in the auld days, that was the kirkyaird o' Ba'weary, and consecrated by the Papists before the blessed licht shone upon the kingdom. It was a great howff o' Mr Soulis's, onyway; there he would sit an' consider his sermons; and indeed it's a bieldy bit. Weel, as he cam' ower the wast end o' the Black Hill ae day, he saw first twa, an' syne fower, an' syne seeven corbie craws fleein' round an' round abune the auld kirky-aird. They flew laigh and heavy, an' squawked to ither as they gaed; and it was clear to Mr Soulis that something had put them frae their ordinar. He wasnae easy fleyed, an' gaed straucht up to the wa's; an' what suld he find there but a man, or the appearance of a man, sittin' in the inside upon a grave. He was of a great stature, an' black as hell, and his e'en were singular to see.* Mr Soulis had heard tell o'black men, mony's the time; but there was something unco about this black man that daunted him. Het as he was, he took a kind o' cauld grue in the marrow o' his banes; but up he spak for a' that; an' says he: "My friend, are you a stranger in this place?" The black man answered never a word; he got upon his feet, an' begude to hirsle to the wa' on the far side; but he aye lookit at the minister; an' the minister stood an' lookit back; till a' in a meenute the black man was ower the wa' an' rinnin' for the bield o' the trees. Mr Soulis, he hardly kenned why, ran after him; but he was sair forjaskit wi' his walk an' the het, unhalesome weather; and rin as he likit, he got nae mair than a glisk o' the black man amang the birks, till he won doun to the foot o' the hillside, an' there he saw him aince mair, gaun hap, step, an' lowp, ower Dule water to the manse.

Mr Soulis wasnae weel pleased that this fearsome gangrel suld mak' sae free wi' Ba'weary manse; an' he ran the harder, an', wet shoon, ower the burn, an' up the walk; but the deil a black man was there to see. He stepped out upon the road, but there was naebody there; he gaed a' ower the gairden, but na, nae black man. At the hinder end, and a bit feared, as was but natural, he lifted the hasp and into the manse; and there was Janet M'Clour before his een, wi' her thrawn craig, and nane sae pleased to see him. And he aye minded sinsyne, when first he set his een upon her, he had the same cauld and deidly grue.

"Janet," says he, "have you seen a black man?"

"A black man?" quo' she. "Save us a'! Ye're no wise, minister. There's nae black man in a' Ba'weary."

But she didnae speak plain, ye maun understand; but yam-yammered, like a powney wi' the bit in its moo.

"Weel," says he, "Janet, if there was nae black man, I have spoken with the Accuser of the Brethren."

And he sat down like ane wi' a fever, an' his teeth chittered in his heid.

"Hoots," says she, "think shame to yoursel', minister," an' gied him a drap brandy that she keepit aye by her.

Syne Mr Soulis gaed into his study amang a' his books. It's a lang, laigh, mirk chalmer, perishin' cauld in winter, an' no very dry even in the tap o' the simmer, for the manse stands near the burn. Sae doun he sat, and thocht of a' that had come an' gane since he was in Ba'weary, an' his hame, an' the days when he was a bairn an' ran daffin' on the braes; and that black man aye ran in his heid like the owercome of a sang. Aye the mair he thocht, the mair he thocht o' the black man. He tried the prayer, an' the words wouldnae

---

*There was a strange, yet common belief in Scotland that the devil appeared as a black man. This appears in several witch trials, and I think in Law's *Memorials*, that delightful storehouse of the quaint and grisly.

come to him, an' he tried, they say, to write at his book, but he couldnae mak' nae mair o' that. There was whiles he thocht the black man was at his oxter, an' the swat stood upon him cauld as well-water; and there was other whiles, when he cam' to himsel' like a christened bairn and minded naething.

The upshot was that he gaed to the window an' stood glowrin' at Dule water. The trees are unco thick, an' the water lies deep an' black under the manse; an' there was Janet washin' the cla'es wi' her coats kilted. She had her back to the minister, an' he, for his pairt, hardly kenned what he was lookin' at. Syne she turned round, an' shawed her face; Mr Soulis had the same cauld grue as twice that day afore, an' it was borne in upon him what folk said, that Janet was deid lang syne, an' this was a bogle in her claycauld flesh. He drew back a pickle and he scanned her narrowly. She was tramp-trampin' in the cla'es, croonin' to hersel'; and eh! Gude guide us, but it was a fearsome face. Whiles she sang louder, but there was nae man born o' woman that could tell the words o' her sang; an' whiles she lookit sidelang doun, but there was naething there for her to look at. There gaed a scunner through the flesh upon his banes; and that was Heeven's advertisement. But Mr Soulis just blamed himsel', he said, to think sae ill of a puir, auld afflicted wife that hadnae a freend forbye himsel'; an' he put up a bit prayer for him and her, an' drank a little caller water—for his heart rose again the meat—an' gaed up to his naked bed in the gloaming.

That was a nicht that has never been forgotten in Ba'weary, the nicht o' the seventeenth of August, seventeen hun'er an' twal'. It had been het afore, as I hae said, but that nicht it was hetter than ever. The sun gaed doun amang unco-lookin' clouds; it fell as mirk as the pit; no a star, no a breath o' wund; ye couldnae see your han' afore your face, and even the auld folk cuist the covers frae their beds and lay pechin' for their breath. Wi' a' that he had upon his mind, it was gey and unlikely Mr Soulis wad get muckle sleep. He lay an' he tummled; the gude, caller bed that he got into brunt his very banes; whiles he slept, and whiles he waukened; whiles he heard the time o' nicht, and whiles a tyke yowlin' up the muir, as if somebody was deid; whiles he thocht he heard bogles claverin' in his lug, an' whiles he saw spunkies in the room. He behoved, he judged, to be sick; an' sick he was—little he jaloosed the sickness.

At the hinder end, he got a clearness in his mind, sat up in his sark on the bedside, and fell thinkin' aince mair o' the black man an' Janet. He couldnae weel tell how—maybe it was the cauld to his feet—but it cam' in upon him wi' a spate that there was some connexion between thir twa, an' that either or baith o' them were bogles. And just at the moment, in Janet's room, which was neist to his, there cam' a stramp o' feet as if men were wars'lin', an' then a loud bang; an' then a wund gaed reishling round the fower quarters of the house; an' then a' was aince mair as seelent as the grave.

Mr Soulis was feared for neither man nor deevil. He got his tinder-box, an' lit a can'le, an' made three steps o't ower to Janet's door. It was on the hasp, an' he pushed it open, an' keeked bauldly in. It was a big room, as big as the minister's ain, an' plenished wi' grand, auld, solid gear, for he had naething else. There was a fower-posted bed wi' auld tapestry; and a braw cabinet of aik, that was fu' o' the minister's divinity books, an' put there to be out o' the gate; an' a wheen duds o' Janet's lying here and there about the floor. But nae Janet could Mr Soulis see; nor ony sign of a contention. In he gaed (an' there's few that wad hae followed him) an' lookit a' round, an' listened. But there was naethin' to be heard, neither inside the manse nor in a' Ba'weary parish, an' naethin' to be seen but the muckle shadows turnin' round the can'le. An' then a' at aince, the minister's heart played dunt an' stood stock-still; an' a cauld wund blew amang the hairs o' his heid. Whaten a weary sicht was that for the puir man's een! For there was Janet hangin' frae a nail beside the auld aik cabinet: her heid aye lay on her shoother, her een were steeked, the tongue projekit frae her mouth, and her heels were twa feet clear abune the floor.

God forgive us all! thocht Mr Soulis, poor Janet's dead.

He cam' a step nearer to the corp; an' then his heart fair whammled in his inside. For by what cantrip it wad ill-beseem a man to judge, she was hingin' frae a single nail an' by a single wursted thread for darnin' hose.

It's an awfu' thing to be your lane at nicht wi' siccan prodigies o' darkness; but Mr Soulis was strong in the Lord. He turned an' gaed his ways oot o' that room, and lockit the door ahint him; and step by step, doon the stairs, as heavy as leed; and set doon the can'le on the table at the stairfoot. He couldnae pray, he couldnae think, he was dreepin' wi' caul' swat, an' naething could he hear but the dunt-dunt-duntin' o' his ain heart. He micht maybe have stood there an hour, or maybe twa, he minded sae little; when a' o' a sudden, he heard a laigh, uncanny steer upstairs; a foot gaed to an' fro in the cha'mer whaur the corp was hingin'; syne the door was opened, though he minded weel that he had lockit it; an' syne there was a step upon the landin', an' it seemed to him as if the corp was lookin' ower the rail and doun upon him whaur he stood.

He took up the can'le again (for he couldnae want the licht), and as saftly as ever he could, gaed straucht out o' the manse an' to the far end o' the causeway. It was aye pit-mirk; the flame o' the can'le, when he set it on the grund, brunt steedy and clear as in a room; naething moved, but the Dule water seepin' and sabbin' doon the glen, an' yon unhaly footstep that cam' ploddin' doun the stairs inside the manse. He kenned the foot ower weel, for it was Janet's; and at ilka step that cam' a wee thing nearer, the cauld got deeper in his vitals. He commended his soul to Him that made an' keepit him; "and, O Lord," said he, "give me strength this night to war against the powers of evil."

By this time the foot was comin' through the passage for the door; he could hear a hand skirt alang the wa', as if the fearsome thing was feelin' for its way. The saughs tossed an' maned thegether, a lang sigh cam' ower the hills, the flame o' the can'le was blawn aboot; an' there stood the corp of Thrawn Janet, wi' her grogram goun an' her black mutch, wi' the heid aye upon the shoother, an' the girn still upon the face o't—leevin', ye wad hae said—deid, as Mr Soulis weel kenned—upon the threshold o' the manse.

It's a strange thing that the saul of man should be that thirled into his perishable body; but the minister saw that, an' his heart didnae break.

She didnae stand there lang; she began to move again an' cam' slowly towards Mr Soulis whaur he stood under the saughs. A' the life o' his body, a' the strength o' his speerit, were glowerin' frae his een. It seemed she was gaun to speak, but wanted words, an' made a sign wi' the left hand. There cam' a clap o' wund, like a cat's fuff; oot gaed the can'le, the saughs skrieghed like folk, an' Mr Soulis kenned that, live or die, this was the end o't.

"Witch, beldame, devil!" he cried, "I charge you, by the power of God, begone—if you be dead, to the grave—if you be damned, to hell."

An' at that moment the Lord's ain hand out o' the Heevens struck the Horror whaur it stood; the auld, deid, desecrated corp o' the witch-wife, sae lang keepit frae the grave and hirsled round by deils, lowed up like a brunstane spunk and fell in ashes to the grund; the thunder followed, peal on dirling peal, the rairing rain upon the back o' that; and Mr Soulis lowped through the garden hedge, and ran, wi' skelloch upon skelloch, for the clachan.

That same mornin' John Christie saw the Black Man pass the Muckle Cairn as it was chappin' six; before eicht, he gaed by the change-house at Knockdow; an' no lang after, Sandy M'Lellan saw him gaun linkin' doun the braes frae Kilmackerlie. There's little doubt but it was him that dwalled sae lang in Janet's body; but he was awa' at last; and sinsyne the deil has never fashed us in Ba'weary.

But it was a sair dispensation for the minister; lang, lang he lay ravin' in his bed; and frae that hour to this, he was the man ye ken the day.

The Three Feathers

Andra Stewart

WELL, oncet upon a time there was a king and this king wis gettin up in years, he wid be away nearly the borders o eighty year auld, ye see, and he took very ill, an he wis in bed. So his doctor come tae see him and . . . he soundit oot the old king lyin in bed, an everything—he come doon, he's asked for the oldest brother tae come, ye see, so he spoke tae the oldest brother, and he says tae the oldest brother, he says: "Yer father hasnae very long tae live," he says, "the best o his days is bye, an," he says, "Ah wouldn't be a bit surprised," says the doctor, "if ye come up some mornin an find him lyin dead in his bed," ye see?

So, of coorse, it wid come as a blow tae the oldest brother, and here, the oldest brother sent for the other two brothers, ye see, sent for Jack and the other two brothers, see? So when the two brothers come up, there wis one o this brothers like, ye understand, they cried him "Silly Jeck", he wis awfae saft and silly, ye know, he widnae dae nothing. He wis a humbug tae the castle; he'd done nothing for the father—in fact he wasnae on the list o gettin ony-thing left when the father died at aw. That wis jist the way o't, ye see. He wis a bad laddie. So anyway, here the three sons is stan'in, the oldest brother tellt them that the father wis goin tae die and something wid have tae be done, and 'at he was goin to be king, ye see. So the good adviser said: "Well," he says, "before the father dies," he says, "he told me that the one that would get the best table-cover, the best an the dearest table-cover that could be found in the country, would get the castle and be king," ye see?

"Well," says the oldest brother, he says. "What are we goin to do," he says, "have we tae go an push wir fortune?"

"No," says the good adviser, he says, "your father gave us three feathers," he says. "Here, they're here," he says, "out of an eagle's wing." An he says, "each o yese got tae take a feather each an go to the top tower o the castle, and throw yer feather up in the air," he says, "an whatever way the feather went, flutter't, that wis the way ye had tae go an push yer fortune for the table-cover."

So right enough they aw agreed, ye see. An Jack wi his guttery boots an everything on—the other yins wis dressed in gaads, ye know, and swords at their side, an Jack jist ploo'ed the fields an scraped the pots doon in the kitchen an everything, cleaned the pots, but Jack wis up wi his guttery boots along wi the rest o the brothers, ye see, an they threw the feathers up, ye see, the two brothers. An one o the feathers went away be the north, the oldest brother's. "Well," he says, "brothers," he says, "see the way my feather went," he says, "away be the north. Ah suppose that'll have to be the way Ah'll have to go an look for the table-cover." The other second oldest brother threw the feather up, and hit went away be the south. "Ah well," he says, "Ah think," he says, "Ah'll have tae go be the south." So poor Jack, they looked at Jack, an they werena gaen tae pey any attention tae Jack, ye see, but Jack threw his feather up an it swirl't roon aboot an it went doon at the back o the castle, in the back-yaird o the castle, ye see? Aw the brothers starit laughin at him: "Ha! ha! ha! ha!" They were makin a fool of Jack, ye see, because his feather went doon at the back o the castle. So Jack gien his shooders a shrug, like that, an he walks doon the stairs, intae the kitchen.

Noo the two brothers, they got a year an a day to get a good table-cover. So Jack never bothered goin to see aboot his table-cover or nothing, ye see, aboot his feather, ye see, so he'd jist aboot a couple o days tae go when the year an the day wis up and Jack's up one day lyin in his bed and he says: "Ma God!" he says, "Ah should go an hae a look at ma feather tae," he says, "Ah've never seen where it wis gettin." It wis a warm kind o afternoon. He says: "Ah'll go for the fun o the thing," he says, "an see where ma feather went." So for curiosity Jack went roon the back o the castle an he wydit through nettles an thistles an he hears a thing goin: "Hoo-ho, o-ho-ho-ho," greetin. Jack looks doon at his feet an here there wis a big green frog sittin, a green puddick, sittin on top o a flagstane, an the tears wis comin out o its een. An Jack looks doon an says: "Whit's wrang wi ye, frog?"

"Oh Jeck, ye didnae gie us much time tae go on tae get ye a table-cover, did ye? Ye should hae been here long ago. You were supposed tae follow yer feather the same as ony ither body."

But Jack says: "I didnae ken," he says, "I thocht . . . when the feather went doon at the back o the castle, Ah jist had tae stay at the castle."

"Oh well, ye cannae help it noo," said the frog, he says, "Ye'd better come away doon. Luft that flagstane," he says. There wis a ring, an iron ring in the flagstane. (Ye know whit a flagstane is? It's a square big stone that's in the ground an ye can lift it up, ye see.) An this big iron ring wis in this flagstane, an Jack wis a big strong lump o a fella, he lifts the stane up aboot half a turn aff the grun, ye see, an there wis trap stairs goin doon. Jack went doon the trap stairs, an the puddick hopped doon the stairs like 'at, an tellt Jack tae mind his feet.

Jack went in. He says: "Well, Ah never seen frogs," he says, "haen a place like this before." A big long passage an 'lectric lights burnin an everything, an frogs goin past him, hoppin past him, an the smell o them eatin, nice smell o restaurant an everything was something terrible, ye see. Took Jack into a lovely place like a parlour, an here when Jack went in he sut doon on this stool, an the frogs aw speakin, speakin tae him, ye see, an one frog jumpit on tap o Jack's knee, an Jack's clappin the wee frog like this, an it's lookin up wi its wee golden eyes, up at Jack's face, an Jack's clappin the wee frog, pattin him on top o the back, an it's lookin up at him an laughin at him in his face.

"Well, Jeck," he says, "you better go now," he says, "ye havenae much time, yer brothers'll be comin home tomorrow," he says, "we'll hae tae get ye a table-cover." So Jack thocht tae hissel, where wis puddicks goin tae get him a table-cover, frogs, ye see, goin tae get a table-cover tae him. But anyway, they come wi a broon paper.

"Now," he says, "Jeck, there is a broon paper parcel," he says, "an there's a cover in there," he says. "Right enough," he says, "yer brothers will have good table-covers, but," he says, "the like o this is no in the country." He says, "Don't open it up," he says, "till you throw it on your father's bed, an when you throw it on your father's bed," he says, "jist tell him tae have a look at that." See?

Jack said, "Aw right."

"Haste up noo, Jeck."

He could hae done wi lookin at the table-cover, but he stuck it 'neath his airm an he bid the wee frogs farewell, an he come up, pit the flagstane doon, an back intae the kitchen. So one o the maids says tae him, "What hae ye got 'neath yer airm, Jeck?" Jack's pitten it up on a shelf, ye see, oot the road.

"Och," he says, "it's ma table-cover," and aw the weemen start laughin, "Ha-ha-ha-ha-ha, silly Jeck gettin a table-cover in his father's castle. You've some hopes o bein king, Jeck." An they never peyed nae attention tae Jack, ye see, so Jack jist never heedit, he's suppin soup wi a spoon, liftin the ladle an suppin, drinkin a ladle oot at a pot, drinkin the soup an everything, ye see.

When he looks up the road, up the great drive, an here comin down is the two brothers comin gallopin their brae steeds, an the medals on their breist an the golden swords, they were glutterin, an here they're comin at an awful speed down the drive, ye see. "Here's ma two brothers comin," an he ran oot the door an he welcomed his two brothers, ye see, an they widnae heed Jack.

"Get oot o ma road," one o them said. "Get oot o ma road, eediot," he says, "you get oot o the road." An they stepped up, ye see, an opened the door an went up tae see their father. So the father said, "There no time the now, sons"—they were greedy, they wantit tae get made king, ye see. . . . "Wait," he says, "until yese get yer dinner, boys," he says, "an then come up an . . . Ah'll see yer table-covers. Ah'll have tae get the good advisers in, ye see." (The good advisers was men. There wis three of them an they pickit whatever wan wis the best, ye see, same as solicitors an things in this days nowadays, ye see.)

So anyway, the two brothers efter they got their feast an everything, their dinner, rung the bells, an here the good advisers come up, red coats on them an they're stan'in beside them. Well, the two sons felt awfy sorry for the old king because he wis gettin very weak an forlorn lookin. He wis ready for tae die any time. "Well, sons," he says. "Well, sons, did yese get the table-covers?"

"Yes," says the oldest son, "Father," he says, "have a look at this table-cover." An he throwed it ower on the bed an they all came an liftit the table-cover, an the father examined the table-cover an it was a lovely, definitely, a lovely silk that ye never seen the like o this table-cover, heavy. Ah couldnae explain whit kind o table-cover this wis.

"Yes," he says, "son," he says, "it definitely is a good table-cover," he says, "an it'll take a bit o beatin. Have you got a table-cover?" he says tae the second youngest son.

"Well," he says, "Father, there's a table-cover," he says. "Ah don't know if it's as good as ma brother's or no," he says, "but have a look at that table-cover." An they looked at the table-cover. Well, the one wis as good as the other. The good advisers couldnae guess which o them wis the best.

"Aw, but hold on," says one—there wis wan o the good advisers likit Jack, ye see. He says, "Hold on," he says, "where's Jeck?"

"Aw," says the other good advisers, "what dae we want with Jeck?"

"Aw, but he's supposed tae be here," he says, "and see if he's got a table-cover," the oldest yin said . . . tae the other good advisers.

So anyway, here now . . . they shouts for Jack and Jack come up the stairs, in his guttery boots as usual, an he's got the broon parcel 'neath his airm. An here the old king says, "Have you got a table-cover, son?" he says.

"Yes, Father," he said, "did ma brothers get the table-covers?"

"Aye," he said, "there they're, there."

"Well," says Jack, he says. "They're definitely nice table-covers, but," he says, "if Ah couldnae get a better table-cover," he says, "than what ma two brothers got," he says, "in yer ain castle, Father," he says, "Ah wadnae go searchin, Ah widnae go," he says. "seekin ma fortune," he says, "the distance they've went," he says, "tae look for table-covers."

So the men start laughin at Jack as usual: "Ha-ha-ha-ha! nonsense. Jeck." An the old king says, "Ah told ye not tae send for him, he's daft," ye see.

"Well," he says, "have a look at that table-cover, Father," so here the father took the scissors and opened the string, an took out . . . . Well, what met their eyes was something terrible. It wis lined with diamonds and rubies, this table-cover. One diamond alone would a' ha' bought the two table-covers that the brothers had, ye see?

"Aye, aye," says the king, "that is a table-cover an a table-covers in time," he says. "Where did ye get it, son? Did ye steal it from some great castle?"

73

"No, Father," he says, "I got this," he says, "in yer own castle."

"It can't be true," says the king, he says: "I've never had a table-cover like that in ma life."

But tae make a long story short, the two brothers wouldnae agree. They said, "Naw, naw, naw, Father," says wan, "that's not fair," he says, "We'll have tae . . . have another chance," ye see. "We'll have tae have another chance," an here they wouldn't let Jack be king. "Aw right," says Jack, "it's all the same tae me," he says, "if yese want a chance again," he says, "very good," he says, "it's aw the same tae me."

So the father says, "Well, if yese want anither chance," he says, "Ah tell ye what Ah want yese tae bring back this time," he says, "an Ah'll give the three of yese a year an a day again," he says. "Seein that Ah'm keepin up in health," he says, "Ah'll give yese another chance. Them 'at'll go an bring back the best ring," he says, " 'll get my whole kingdom," he says, ye see, "when Ah die."

Well, fair enough. The three brothers went an got their feathers again and went tae the top of the tower. The oldest brother threw his feather up an it went away be the east. "Aw well," he says, "it'll have tae be me away for east." The other brother threw a feather up—the secondest youngest brother, an it went away be the south. "Aw well," says the other brother, he says, "Ah'll go away be the south." Jack threw his feather up, but they didnae laugh this time. It swirl't roon aboot like that an it went doon the back o the castle, in amongst the nettles an the thistles. So they looked, the two brothers looked at each other but they never said a word. They jist went doon the stair an Jack follae't them the big tower, ye see, doon the steps. (Stone steps in them days in the old castles.) And the two brothers bid farewell, mountit their horses and they're away for all they can gallop in each direction, waved tae each other wi their hands an away they went. Ye could see them goin ower the horizon, see?

Jack never bother't, ye see. He went down an he's two or three month in the hoose an oot he went roon. An he seen the same thing happen't again, he went roond the back o the castle an here's the frog sittin on tap o the flag-stane. "Aye," he says, "Jeck, ye're back quicker this time," he says. "What did ye think of the table-cover?"

"Och," he says, "it wid hae bought ma faither's castle althegither, right oot be the root."

"Aye," he says, "Ah tellt it wis a good table-cover," he says. "Now," he says, "Ah'll have tae get ye a ring," says the frog. "Ye better come away doon an see the rest o the family," ye see? Lifts the flagstane up an Jack went doon the steps, ye see, an intae this big parlour place an he's sittin down, the 'lectric lights is burnin, an this wee frog jumped on tap o his knee an he's aye clappin this wee frog, ye see, on tap o his knee, clappin the wee frog, an it's croakin up in his face wi its wee golden eyes, ye see. Well, they gien him a good meat, ye know, no frogs' meat or onything like that, it wis good meat they gien him on dishes, this frogs hoppin aboot the place an gien him a nice feed, ye see, an they gies him this wee box—it wis a velvet box, black, did ye ever see wee black velvet boxes? He says, "There it is, Jeck," he says, "an the like of that ring," he says, "is not in the country," he says. "Take it tae yer father an let him see that."

So Jack stuck it in his waistcoat pocket—an auld waistcoat he had on, ye see, an he's oot, an he's cleanin—but he wis forgettin aboot the year an the day—it passed quicker, ye see. Here's the two brothers comin doon the avenue on their great horses, galloping. Jumped aff an said, "Did ye get. . . ." They wantit tae ken if Jack got a ring.

Jack says, "Look," he says, "dinnae bother me," says Jack, he says. "Go up an see the aul man," he says, "instead o goin lookin for rings," he said. "Ah've never seen as much nonsense as this in ma life." He says, "Why can they no let you be king," he says, "onywey, ye're the oldest," he says, "'stead o cairryin on like this."

"Oh," he says, "what's tae be done is tae be done, Jeck," so away they went, up tae see their father. The good advisers wis there. And they showed the rings tae their father, an the father's lookin at the two rings, an judgin the rings, oh, they were lovely rings, no mistake about it, they were lovely rings, ye see, diamonds an everything on them. Here they come—Jack come up the stair again an he wabbles in an he's lookin at them arguin aboot the rings and Jack says, "Look, Father," he says, "have a look at that ring." Jack never seen the ring, and the father opened the wee box and what met his eyes, it hurtit the good advisers' an the old king's eyes, it hurted them. There wis a stone, a diamond stone, sittin in it—would have bought the whole castle an the land right about it, ye see?

So anyway, here the brothers widnae be pleased at this. "Naw, naw, naw, this is nae use, Father," says wan, "give us another chance," he says. "The third time's a charm," he says, "give us another chance."

"But," says the father, he says, "Jeck won twice," he says, "it's no fair," an the good adviser, the old man 'at like Jack said, "No, no, Jeck'll have to be king. He won twice."

"No, no, Father, gie us another chance," says wan. So the brother says, "Ah'll tell ye, Father, let us get a good wife," he says, "tae fit the ring an them that gets the nicest bride tae fit the ring'll get the king's castle. How will that do, Jeck?"

Jack says, "Fair enough tae me." But Jack got feart noo because he mindit it wis puddicks he wis amongst. Where would he get a wife from amongst a lot o wee puddicks, frogs an things, ye see? Same thing again, up tae the tap o the tower an threw off their feathers, and one feather went away one road and the other feather went away the other road, but Jack's feather went roon tae the back o the castle. "Aw," says Jack, "Ah'm no going back. That's it finished now, Jeck." Jack says, "Ah'm lowsed." He says, "Ah'm no goin tae tak nae wee frog for a wife," ye see?

So anyway, Jack waited tae the year wis up, an jist for the fun o the thing, he says, "Ah'll go roond the back o the castle," he says, "an see what's goin 'ae happen." Roon he went tae the back o the castle and here's three or four frogs sittin greetin, and the wee frog that sut on his knee, hit wis greetin, the tears runnin out o its een, an it wis jist like a man playin pibroch, "Hee-haw, hee-haw", an aw the frogs is greetin, ye see, an here all danced wi glee, and this wee frog come an met him an looked up in his face and climbed up his leg, this wee tottie frog, an he lifted the flagstane an they hoppit doon, ye see?

"Well, Jeck," the old frog says to Jack, he says, "Ah wis thinkin," he says, "Jeck, ye widnae come," he says. "Ye were frightened," he says, "we couldnae get ye a wife, didn't ye Jeck?"

"Yes," says Jack, "tae be truthful wi ye," he says, "I thought," he says, "a frog," he says, "widnae do me for a wife."

"Well," says the old man, efter they gied him somethin tae eat, he says, "How wid ye like Susan for a wife?" An this wis the wee frog that wis on his knee, an he wis clappin it.

Jack says, "That wee frog," he says, "how could that make a wife tae me?"

"Yes, Jeck," he says, "that is yer wife," he says, "an a woman," he says, "a wife," he says, "yer brothers," he says, "will have pretty women back wi them," he says, "but nothing like Susan."

So anyway, here, they says, "Go out," to Jack, "Go out for an hour," he says, "round the back," he says, "an intae the kitchen," he says, "and take a cup o tea an come back out again," he says; "we'll have everything ready for ye." Jack went roond noo an he's feared, he didn't know what wis gonnae tae happen, an he's taken a cup o tea, but he's back roond.

Here when he come roon at the back o the castle beside the trees, there wis a great big cab sittin, lined wi gold, an the wee frog, it wis the frog, was the loveliest princess ever ye seen in yer life. She wis dressed in silk, ye could see through the silk that wis on her—she wis jist a walkin spirit, a lovely angel she looked like, an when Jack seen her, he says, wi his guttery boots an everything, he wouldn't go near her. So this old king, it wis an old king, a fat frog wi a big belly, green, an he says, "There is yer bride, there's Susan," he says. "How dae ye like the look o her, Jeck?"

Jack rubbed his eyes like that. . . . He says, "Look," he says, "Ah couldnae take a lady like that," he says. He says, "it's impossible. . . . Look at the mess Ah'm in."

"Oh but," says the puddicks, they says, "we'll soon pit that right," says the old frog, and he says, "jist turn three times roon aboot," an Jack turned three times: an as he's turnin roon aboot his claes wis changin, an there he's turned the beautifullest king ye ever seen in yer life—a prince, medals an a gold sword—ye never seen the like o it in yer life, an this cab wi six grey horses in it and footmen an everything on the back o the cab, an here when she seen Jack she come an put her airms roon Jack's neck, an Jack kissed her, ye see, an they went intae the cab.

Now they drove oot—this wis the year an a day up now, ye see, this was the term's day—but when they come roon here they're comin drivin up the road, but the two brothers wis up before Jack, an . . . they sees the cab comin up the drive, an the two brothers looked oot the windae, an "Aw, call out the guard," they said, an here's the guard out and the old king got up oot o his bed, he's lookin through the windae, opened the big sash curtains back, an he says, "Ah told ye," he says, "Jeck stole the ring an stole the table-cover. This is the king come," he says, "tae . . . claim his goods," he says, "that Jeck stole."

Well anyway, here, what happens but the two brothers cam oot an they says, "Oh," they says, "Ah told ye, Father, not tae take Jeck," but here when Jack stepped oot o the cab and they seen Jack, Jack waved up tae the windae, his father, "Hi Dad!" he says, an he shouts tae his father. The father looked doon an he rubbed his een an he says, "Is that you, Jeck?"

Jack says, "Yes, Father, it's me," he says, "an here is ma wife. Ah'm comin up tae see ye."

Well, when the two brothers seen Jack's wife they went an took their two wives an they pit them intae the lavatories an locked the door. Haud them oot o the road, intae the lavatories they pit them. "Get away oot o here, shoo, get oot o here, get oot o here! Oh, Jeck's wife," says wan, "we wouldn't be shamed wi youse women!" An the two lassies that the two oldest brothers had started tae cry, ye see, they shoved them intae the lavatories. "Go in there," wan says, "oot o the road," he says, "until I get ye a horse," he says, "that ye can gallop away."

An when Jack come up an . . . when the father an the good advisers seen this lovely princess, the like wis never in the country, they made Jack king, and the bells were ringin for the feast an Jack was the king. An he wis good to aw the poor folk aw roon the country, folk 'at the owld king used tae be good to, Jack wis three times better tae them an they loved Jack for ever after, an Jack lived happy, an he's king noo on the tap o Keelymabrook, away up in the hills.

That's the end o ma story.

The Blot

Iain Crichton Smith

MISS Maclean said, "And pray tell me how did you get the blot on your book?"

I stood up in my seat automatically and said, "It was . . . I put too much ink in the pen, please, miss." I added again forlornly, "Please, miss." She considered or seemed to consider this for a long time, but perhaps she wasn't really thinking about it at all, perhaps she was thinking about something else. Then she said, "And did you not perhaps think of putting less ink in your pen? I imagine one has a choice in those matters." The rest of the class laughed as they always did, promptly and decorously, whenever Miss Maclean made a joke. She said, "Be quiet", and they stopped laughing as if one of the taps mentioned in our sums had been switched off. Miss Maclean always wore a grey thin blouse and a thin black jacket. Sometimes she seemed to me to look like a pencil.

"Do you not perhaps believe in having a tidy book as the rest of us do?" she said. I didn't know what to say. Naturally I believed in having a tidy book. I liked the whiteness of a book more than anything else in the world. To write on a white page was like . . . how can I say it? . . . it was like a bird leaving footprints in snow. But then to say that to her was to sound daft. And anyway, why couldn't she clean the globe which lay in front of her on the desk? It was always dusty so that you could leave your fingerprints all over Europe or South America or Antigua. Antigua was a really beautiful name; I had come across it recently in an atlas. The highest mark she ever gave for an essay was five out of ten, and she was always spoiling jotters by filling them with comments and scoring through words and adding punctuation marks. But I must admit that when she wrote on the board she wrote very neatly.

"And what's this," she said, "about an old woman? I thought you were supposed to write about a postman. Have you never seen a postman?" She was always asking stupid questions like that. Of course I had seen a postman. "And what's this word 'solatary'? I presume you mean 'solitary'. You shouldn't use big words unless you can spell them. And whoever saw an old woman peering out through the letter-box when the postman came up the stairs? You really have the oddest notions." The class laughed again. No, I had not actually seen an old woman peering through a letter-box, but there was no reason why one shouldn't, why my old woman shouldn't. In fact she *had* been peering through the letter-box. I was angry at having misspelt "solitary". I didn't know how I had come to do that, since I knew the correct spelling. "Old women don't look through letter-boxes waiting for letters," she almost screamed, her face reddening with rage.

Why did she hate me so much? I wondered. It was the same when I wrote the essay about the tiger who ate fish and chips. Was it really because my work wasn't neat and because I was always putting ink-blots on the paper? My hands were clumsy, there was no getting away from that. They never did what I wanted them to do. Her hands, however, were very thin and neat, ringless. Not like my mother's hands. My mother's hands were wrinkled and one of the fingers had a plain gold ring which she could never get off.

"Old women don't spend their time waiting for letters," she shouted. "They have other things to do with their time. I have never seen an old woman who waited every day for a letter. Have you? HAVE you?"

I thought for some time and then said, "No, miss."

"Well then," she said, breathing less heavily. "But you always want to be clever, don't you? I asked you to write about a postman and you write about an old woman. That is impertinence. ISN'T IT?"

I knew what I was expected to answer so I said, "Yes, miss."

She looked down at the page from an enormous height with her thin hawk-like gaze and read out a sentence in a scornful voice. " 'She began to write a letter to herself but as she did so a blot of ink fell on the page and she stopped.' Why did you write that? That again is deliberate insolence."

"It came into my mind at that . . . after I had put the ink on my jotter. It just came into my head."

"It was insolence, wasn't it? WASN'T IT?"

Actually it hadn't been. It had been a kind of inspiration. The idea came into my head very quickly and I had written the sentence before I thought how it would appear to her. I hadn't been thinking of her when I was writing the composition. But from now on I would have to think of her, I realised. Whatever I wrote I would have to think of her reading it and the thought filled me with despair. I couldn't understand why her face quivered with rage when she spoke to me, why she showed such hatred. I didn't want to be hated. Who wanted to be hated like this?

I felt this even while she was belting me. Perhaps she was right. Perhaps it had been insolence. Perhaps neatness was the most important thing in the world. After she had belted me she might be kind to me again and she might stop watching me all the time as if I was an enemy. The thing was, I must learn to hide from her, be neat and clean. Maybe that would work, and her shouting would go away. But even as I thought that and was writhing with pain from the belt, I was also thinking, Miss Maclean, very clean, Miss Maclean, very clean. The words shone without my bidding in front of my head. I was always doing that. Sums, numbs, bums, mums. I also thought, Have you Macleaned your belt today? I thought of a story where a dirty old man, a tramp sitting by the side of the road, would shout, "Why aren't you as clean as me?" The tramp was very like old Mackay who worked on the roads and was always singing hymns, while breaking the rock. And there was another story where the belt would stand up like a snake and sway to music. In front of her thin grey blouse the belt would rise, with a snake's head and a green skin. I could even hear the accompanying music, staccato and vibrant. It was South American music and came from the dusty globe in front of her.

Jimmy and the Policeman

Iain Crichton Smith

T HERE was once in our village an unpopular policeman and a pickpocket. When I say that the policeman was unpopular I mean that he was far too energetic to be a good village policeman and he was also too thin. Most village policemen are fat large men with red faces, who usually have their tunics open and pace steadfastly like comics from a film. They will pass the time of day with the locals, pretend that the bar has actually shut at ten o'clock on the dot, discuss gardening, lean over fences, and generally leave the villagers to mind their own business. This particular policeman wasn't like that at all. First of all he was, as I have said, very thin, and secondly he was determined to clamp down on all crime, and thirdly he didn't want to be outwitted by anyone.

He would call at the bar at ten o'clock to make sure that everyone had stopped drinking. He interfered in the Case of the Missing Cow, and made a mess of things. After all, if he had left the affair alone, everyone would have been quite happy, but he had to stir things up. And in any case the cow hadn't been stolen at all. He even bothered the children and there was the Case of the Green and Red Marbles which I shall not trouble you with because it was so trivial. Thus it was decided that since in a village everyone must make allowances for everyone else, he should be taught a lesson. And the instrument which destiny chose was Jimmy Smith, a pickpocket. But again let me qualify this. Jimmy was not a criminal, he was a joker. He had quick hands but he used them to entertain people. He was an independent little man with a great dislike for authority of any kind. There was an element of the child in his nature and he liked best to play with the children with whom he would make balloons disappear, handkerchiefs end up in the wrong pockets, and marbles change colour like those sweets they used to call bull's-eyes.

Now the policeman took an instinctive dislike to him because I suppose he puzzled him. Jimmy had no interest in money or getting on in the world. He did odd jobs for people but otherwise seemed perfectly happy where he was, puffing at his pipe all day. He had a small black pipe with a silver lid on it which was his most precious possession. Most of the day he would sit in front of the door, playing with pebbles which he had picked up, or sitting in his room reading a book. He was a great reader and was never more content than when he was immersed in an old Western or a ragged detective story that had gone the rounds of the village. Nevertheless, though he was harmless, the policeman was suspicious of him—partly, I think, because he was so indolent and there was no way in which power could be exerted over him, and partly because there was a peculiar creative streak in his nature which the policeman found disturbing. Once he tried to get him for drinking, but in some unaccountable manner Jimmy disappeared and the policeman couldn't nail him at all.

One day he came to Jimmy's house and spoke to him in the following terms.

"Jimmy," he said, "I'm the policeman in this village and I want you to understand this. I'm determined to be a good one. That is to say, no crime will be permitted here while I am the policeman. I have the feeling that you are secretly laughing at me and I won't have it. I have heard certain things you have said about me, joking references, and I won't put up with them."

"Oh, excuse me a moment," said Jimmy, who seemed hardly to be listening, "while I make a cup of tea. I wonder if perhaps you would like one."

"I. . . ."

Now, it happened that it was rather a hot day and the policeman was feeling sticky in his warm blue uniform, so thinking that he would make himself look human—for he wasn't a complete fool—he agreed to accept a cup of tea. Another reason why he accepted the tea was that he wished to have more time to look at Jimmy and study him. Jimmy was apparently unconcerned but bustled about with cups and saucers. The policeman gazed idly round the room, which was neat and tidy and small. There didn't seem to be enough space, as they say, to swing a cat. There was a sink at which Jimmy was busy, there were two chairs, a fireplace which was completely bare, a small cooker, a table and nothing else. Jimmy, it seemed, was a spiritual monk as far as possessions were concerned. There was, however, a big red balloon hanging from the middle of the ceiling and a guitar in one corner. All the time, Jimmy bustled about with his pipe in his mouth. It was noticeable that sometimes he didn't smoke at all, though he still kept the pipe between his teeth.

When the tea was ready Jimmy took the cups over and laid them down on— oh yes, I forgot, there was a stool. All the time, he had been talking in some mysterious way, for he still had the pipe in his mouth, saying that he had nothing against the policeman, that all he wanted was to be left alone, that he wished he could play the guitar better, that it was a fine day, that someone's cow had been eating his washing, that he had just finished a comic song which . . . . But the funny thing was that when he laid the cups down, somehow or other, either by accident or design, the tea from one of the cups was spilt over the policeman. The latter got up in a rage while Jimmy dabbed at him with a cloth which he had taken over from the sink, his hands flying hither and thither, faster it seemed than lightning and at one time whipping out the policeman's handkerchief to help repair the damage. All this time he kept up a running fire of apologies while the policeman's face reddened and reddened. Eventually the trousers were dried out by means of the cloth and the handkerchief, and the policeman was about to storm out, still swearing vengeance against Jimmy who appeared entirely anguished and staggered by what had happened and was suggesting that the policeman should have another cup of tea. However, the latter, not to be mollified, prepared to leave, renewing his pose, ready to confront the world again, dry and complete.

However, just as he was leaving, Jimmy said quietly, "I wonder if you have still got the five pound note you keep in your wallet." The policeman looked at him, saw some dancing glitter of comedy in his eyes, took out his wallet and sure enough there was a five pound note missing.

There was a long silence in the room interrupted only by the frantic buzzing of a bluebottle against dim panes. The two men gazed at each other. The balloon swung gently between them and the guitar leaned back in its corner.

"So," said the policeman at last, "this is a challenge." He brooded for a moment, thought that beating Jimmy up was not on, that pure deduction must be the answer, that if he didn't come up with the answer he was finished in the village, and then proceeded to think. Jimmy glanced at him mockingly. For the first time the policeman realised that there was an elfin quality about Jimmy, in the thin ironic face, and the playful smile, that he had too what could only be called an implacable cheek. He said, "First of all I have to search you. Come here."

Jimmy submitted to the search in a good-humoured manner, but there was not a five pound note on him. There was no money on him at all.

The policeman took a walk over to the sink. There was nothing there either. It was neat and tidy and white. The policeman examined himself. There were no five pound notes in his pockets and nothing in his turn-ups. He opened the wallet again to make sure that the money hadn't been returned there in some mysterious manner, but it hadn't. He looked in the fireplace, but that was bare. He tried the top of the stool, but it remained fixed. He made Jimmy stand naked while he examined all his clothes. For one terrifying moment he thought that perhaps Jimmy had gambled on this, that he would have arranged for someone to be watching, and that he, the policeman, would be accused of sodomy. He made Jimmy put on his clothes again. Jimmy sat back in the chair, puffing at his pipe contentedly. The policeman gazed at him. He said at last, "I am really a very good policeman, you know. It would be a tragedy for you if I were to leave. Who else would you get in my place but some idiot who would be unable to solve any of your crimes? I believe in what I am doing. I was born to be a policeman. You think your idyllic existence will go on for ever, that there will never be any serious crime or murder. But how do you know that? All you have to do is read the papers."

The silent guitar leaned back in the corner. The balloon drifted a little, like someone breathing. Jimmy said nothing but smiled. The policeman knew that if Jimmy told the story of the Locked Room he would never recover from it. In a sudden rage he pulled down the balloon and burst it as if he thought the money might be inside it, but it wasn't, and the deflated balloon lay on the floor. He searched in the teapot and the kettle, but there was nothing there. He looked in the tin where the tea had been.

"I've got it!" he said at last. "I know what you've done. I know exactly what you've done. You've rolled the money up and put it in your pipe bowl." Jimmy looked at him in wonderment and slightly fearfully. He mimicked alarm and despondency. He seemed to protest as he handed the pipe over. The policeman looked into the bowl. There was nothing there.

He sat and looked at Jimmy in despair. He had tried everything and he hadn't found the solution. The room was small and bare. There were no other hiding-places.

For the first time, however, he realised that there was a clock and that it was ticking rather loudly. He felt that it was ticking away his career. He remembered the stories about Jimmy, how once at Hallowe'en he had made a cart disappear, how he could do weird things with telephones. . . . As he sat there in amazement and bafflement, Jimmy said, "You're a good policeman. You're really very good. But what you haven't realised is that if you go on the way you are going you will increase and not decrease the amount of crime in the village. You will have to learn to leave people alone unless there is something really serious. Look at me. I leave people alone. I'm cleverer than you. I've just proved it. My mind works faster. If I wanted to commit a serious crime I could get away with it. You have forced me to take a five pound note from you. That is a crime you are directly responsible for. Do you understand? Now, I am a law-abiding person, and if the law were just I should be able to sue you for serious temptation, but I am not going to sue you. I'm letting you off. Do you realise that I have put you in prison? This room is a prison for you. You can't leave it because I have wound round you a net of the mind. For years, for the rest of your life, if you leave now with the mystery unsolved, you will be wondering about it. It will cause self-doubt. You will never be the policeman you were. I hope you understand that clearly."

The policeman looked at him for a long time and then said, "You are saying that you are offering me a bargain."

"Yes. The fact that you thought of my pipe suggests that you are clever. You will have to learn to be tolerant. Will you do that if I tell you the solution?"

"Yes," said the policeman at long last. "I'll do that. I have understood everything you have said."

"Good," said Jimmy springing up. "The five pound note is pinned to the back of your tunic. If you had gone out of this house swearing vengeance on me with the five pound note pinned to your tunic, what do you think would have happened?"

The policeman shivered as if in a cold wind.

"Now," said Jimmy, "I think we'll have a proper cup of tea. Or rather, whisky. I make it myself, you know. After all we have something to celebrate. The return of a policeman to ordinary humanity."

Five Green Waves

George Mackay Brown

1

TIME was lines and circles and squares.

"You will go home at once to your father," said Miss Ingsetter, rapping her desk with a ruler, "and tell him I sent you, because you have not prepared the mathematics lesson I told you to prepare. Now go!"

A rustle went through the class-room. The pupils looked round at me, wide-eyed. A few made little sorrowing noises with their lips. For it was a terrible punishment. My father was a magnate, a pillar of authority in the island—Justice of the Peace, Kirk Elder, Registrar, Poor Inspector, a member of the Education Committee itself. He was, in addition, the only merchant in the place and kept the shop down by the pier; even before I was born he had decided that his boy would be a credit to him—he would go to the university and become a minister, or a lawyer, or a doctor.

Now, this summer afternoon, while bluebottles like vibrant powered ink-blobs gloried in the windows and the sun came four-square through the burning panes, my stomach turned to water inside me.

"Please, Miss Ingsetter," I said, "I'm sorry I didn't learn the theorem. I promise it won't happen again. I would be glad if you punished me yourself."

The bust of Shelley gazed at me with wild blank eyes.

Her spectacles glinted. Down came the ruler with a snap. "You will go to your father, now, at once, and tell him of your conduct."

The bright day fell in ruins about me. I crossed the floor on fluttering bare feet, and was soon outside.

"You, Willie Sinclair," I heard her shouting through the closed door, "stand up and give us the theorem of Pythagoras."

A red butterfly lighted on my hand, clung there for a moment, and went loitering airily across the school garden, now here among the lupins, now there over the flowering potatoes, as if it was drunk with happiness and didn't know on what bright lip to hang next. I watched it till it collapsed over the high wall, a free wind-tipsy flower.

Inside the class-room, the formal wave gathered and broke.

". . . is equal to the sum of the squares on the other two sides," concluded Willie Sinclair in a sibilant rush.

"Very good, Willie," said Miss Ingsetter.

Despised and rejected, I turned for home.

2

The croft of Myers stands beside the road, looking over the Sound, and the hill rises behind it like a swelling green wave. Sophie, a little bent woman, her grey shawl about her head, was throwing seed to the twelve hens.

She smelt me on the wind. "Hello there," she cried. I muttered a greeting. She peered at me. "And who might you be?" she said.

I told her my name.

"Mercy," she said, "but you've grown."

Our voices had roused the old man inside. He was suddenly at the door, smiling. Peter's face was very red and round. He had been a sailor in his youth. The backs of his hands, and his wrists, smouldered with blue anchors, blue mermaids, blue whales. "Come in," he cried.

It was like entering a ship's hold, but for the smells of peat and kirn and girdle. I breathed darkness and fragrance.

They ushered me to the straw chair beside the fire. I had hardly got settled in it when Sophie put a bowl of ale between my hands. The sweet heavy fumes drifted across my nostrils.

Peter sat filling his pipe in the other straw chair. The old woman never rested for an instant. She moved between the fire and the window and the bed, putting things in order. She flicked her duster along the mantelpiece, which was full of tea-caddies and ships in bottles. The collie dog lolled and panted on the flagstones.

"And tell me," said Peter, "what way you aren't at school?"

"I got sent home," I said, "for not learning the lesson."

"You must learn your lessons," said Sophie, setting the fern straight in the tiny window. "Think what way you'll be in thirty years' time if you don't, a poor ignorant fellow breaking stones in the quarry."

I took a deep gulp of ale, till my teeth and tongue and palate were awash in a dark seething wave.

"And tell me," said Peter, "what will you be when you're big?"

"A sailor," I said.

"If that wasn't a splendid answer!" cried Peter. "A sailor. Think of that."

"My grandfather was a gunner on the *Victory*," said Sophie. "He was at Trafalgar. He came home with a wooden leg."

"That was great days at sea," said Peter. "Do you know the Ballad of Andrew Ross?"

"No," I said.

A hen, shaped like a galleon, entered from the road outside. She dipped and swayed round the sleeping dog, and went out again into the sunlight.

"Woman," said Peter, "get the squeeze-box."

Sophie brought a black dumpy cylinder from under the bed, and blew a spurt of dust from it. Peter opened the box and took out a melodeon.

"Listen," he said. A few preliminary notes as sharp as spray scattered out of the instrument. Then he cleared his throat and began to sing:

> "Andrew Ross an Orkney sailor
> Whose sufferings now I will explain
> While on a voyage to Barbados,
> On board the good ship *Martha Jane*."

"That was the name of the ship," said Sophie, "the *Martha Jane*."
"Shut up," said Peter.

> "The mates and captain daily flogged him
> With whips and ropes, I tell you true,
> Then on his mangled bleeding body
> Water mixed with salt they threw."

"That's what they used to do in the old days, the blackguards," said Sophie. "They would beat the naked backs of the sailors till they were as red as seaweed."

"Damn it," said Peter, "is it you that's reciting this ballad, or is it me?"

> "The captain ordered him to swallow
> A thing whereof I shall not name.
> The sailors all grew sick with horror.
> On board the good ship *Martha Jane*."

"What was it Andrew Ross had to swallow?" I asked.

"It was too terrible to put in the song," said Sophie.

"I'll tell you what it was," said Peter, glaring at me. "It was *his own dung*."

The sickness began to work like a yeast in the region of my throat. I took a big swallow of ale to drown it.

Peter sang:

> "When nearly dead they did release him,
> And on the deck they did him fling.
> In the midst of his pain and suffering
> 'Let us be joyful,' Ross did sing."

"He was religious," said Sophie, "and the captain was an atheist. That's the way they bad-used him."

> "The captain swore he'd make him sorry,
> And jagged him with an iron bar.
> Was not that a cruel treatment
> For an honoured British tar!"

The house took a long dizzy lurch to starboard, then slowly righted itself. My knuckle grew white on the edge of the chair. The good ship Myers burrowed again into the fluid hill.

"Mercy," said Sophie, "I doubt the boy's too young for a coarse ballad like that."

> "Justice soon did overtake them
> When into Liverpool they came.
> They were found guilty of the murder
> Committed on the briny main."

"High time too," said Sophie. "The vagabonds!"

> "Soon the fateful hour arrived
> That Captain Rogers had to die,
> To satisfy offended justice
> And hang on yonder gallows high."

I stood erect on the heaving flagstones. "Going to be sick," I said.

"The pail!" cried Sophie, "where's the pail?"

But she was too late. Three strong convulsions went through me, and I spouted thrice. The flagstones were awash. The dog barked. Then the cottage slowly settled on an even keel, and I was sitting in the straw chair, my eyes wet with shame and distress. Not even Andrew Ross's sorrow was like unto my sorrow.

Old Sophie was on her knees with a wet clout and a bucket.

Peter patted me on the shoulder. "Don't you worry," he said. "You're not the first sailor that's been sick on his maiden voyage."

3

Below the kirkyard the waves stretched long blue necks shoreward. Their manes hissed in the wind, the broken thunder of their hoofs volleyed along the beach and echoed far inland among cornfields and peatbogs and trout lochs, and even as far as the quiet group of standing stones at the centre of the island.

I made my way shoreward, walking painfully along a floor of round pebbles.

One had to be careful; Isaac of Garth, going home drunk and singing on Saturday nights, was in the habit of smashing his empty bottles on these rocks. He had done it for so many years that the amphitheatre of pebbles above the sand was dense with broken glass—the older fragments worn by the sea to blunt opaque pebbles, the newer ones winking dangerously in the sun. If one of the sharp pieces scored your foot, you might easily bleed to death.

There was no one in sight along the wide curve of the beach, or on the road above. In the kirkyard the grave-digger was up to the hips in a grave he was making for Moll Anderson, who had died at the week-end.

Quickly and cautiously, under a red rock, I took off my clothes—first the grey jersey with the glass button at the neck, next the trousers made out of an old pair of my father's, and finally the blue shirt. Then I ran down to the sea and fell through an incoming wave. Its slow cold hammer drove the air out of my lungs. I thrashed through the water to a rock thirty yards out and clung to it, gasping and shivering. Lord, I thought, suppose Miss Ingsetter or my father saw me now! A shred of cloud raced across the sun, and the world plunged in and out of gloom in a second. And then, for an hour, I was lost in the cry and tumult of the waves. Shags, dark arrows, soared past my plunging face. Gulls cut gleaming arcs and circles against the sky, and traversed long corridors of intense sound. Seals bobbed up and down like bottles in the Sound, and grew still every now and then when I whistled. For a brief eternity I was lost in the cry, the tumult, the salt cleansing ritual of the sea.

The grave-digger paused in his work and, shading his eyes beachward, saw me stumbling out of the waves. He shook his fist at my nakedness. The sand was as hot as new pancakes under my feet. I ran wild and shouting up the beach and fell gasping on my heap of clothes. I lay there for a long time. From very far away, on the other side of the hill, a dog barked. The rockpool shimmered in the heat. The music of the grave-digger's spade rang bright and fragile across the field. Suddenly three words drifted from the rock above me: "You naked boy." I looked up into the face of Sarah, Abraham the tinker's daughter. She rarely came to school, but whenever she did she sat like a wild creature under the map of Canada. She was sprawling now on the rock with her legs dangling over. Her bare arms and her thighs, through the red torn dress she wore, were as brown as an Indian's.

Sarah said, "I come here every day to watch the boats passing. When the sun goes down tonight we're moving to the other end of the island. There's nothing there but the hill and the hawk over it. Abraham has the lust for rabbits on him."

The tinkers have curious voices—angular, outcast, flashing accents like the cries of seagulls.

She jumped down from the rock and crouched in front of me. I had never seen her face so close. Her hair lay about it in two blue-black whorls, like mussel shells. Her eyes were as restless as tadpoles, and her small nose shone as if it had been oiled.

"Sarah," I said, "you haven't been to school all week."

"May God keep me from that place for ever," she said.

With quick curious fingers she began to pick bits of seaweed out of my hair.

"What will you do," she said, "when you're a tall man? You won't live long, I can tell that. You'll never wear a gold chain across your belly. You're white like a mushroom." She laid two dirty fingers against my shoulder.

"I'm going to be a sailor," I said, "or maybe an explorer."

She shook her head slowly. "You couldn't sleep with ice in your hair," she said.

"I'll take to the roads with a pack then," I said, "for I swear to God I don't want to be a minister or a doctor. I'll be a tinker like you."

She shook her head again. "Your feet would get broken, tramping the roads we go," she said.

Her red dress fell open at the shoulder where the button had come out of it. Her shoulder shone in the wind as if it had been rubbed with sweet oils.

She stretched herself like an animal and lay down on the sand with her eyes closed.

I turned away from her and traced slow triangles and circles in the sand. I turned a grey stone over; a hundred forky-tails seethed from under it like thoughts out of an evil mind. From across the field came the last chink of the grave-digger's spade—the grave was dug now; the spade leaned, miry and glittering, against the kirkyard wall. Two butterflies, red and white over the rockpool, circled each other in silent ecstasy, borne on the stream of air. They touched for a second, then fell apart, flickering in the wind, and the tall grass hid them. I turned quickly and whispered in Sarah's ear.

Her first blow took me full in the mouth. She struck me again on the throat as I tried to get to my feet. Then her long nails were in my shoulder and her wild hair fell across my face. She thrust me back until my shoulder-blades were in the burning sand and my eyes wincing in the full glare of the sun. She dug sharp knees into my ribs until I screamed. Then she ravelled her fingers through my hair and beat my head thrice on the hard sand. Through my shut lids the sun was a big shaking gout of blood.

At last she let me go. "Next time I come to the school," she said, looking down at me with dark smiling eyes, "I'll sit at your desk, under the yellow head of the poet." She bent over quickly and held her mouth against my throat for as long as it takes a wave to gather and break. Her hair smelt of ditch-water and grass fires. Then she was gone.

I put on the rest of my clothes, muttering through stiff lips, "You bitch! O you bloody bully, I'll have the attendance officer after you in ten minutes, just see if I don't!"

As I left the beach, walking slowly, I could see her swimming far out in the Sound.

She waved and shouted, but I turned my face obstinately towards the white road that wound between the kirkyard and the cornfield. The salt taste of blood was in my mouth.

The grave-digger had finished making Moll Anderson's grave. He was sitting on the shaft of his barrow, smoking a clay pipe. As I turned in at the gate he wagged his beard at me, for he did not associate this shy decently clad boy with the naked insolence he had seen running out of the sea half an hour before. I wandered away from him among the branching avenues of tomb-stones—the tall urns and frozen angels of modern times; the fiery pillars with the names of grandfathers on them; the scythe-and-hourglass slates of the eighteenth century; and the lichened leprous tombs of a still earlier age. This small field was honeycombed with the dead of generations—farmers with stony faces; young girls rose-cheeked with consumption; infants who had sighed once or twice and turned back to the darkness; stern Greek-loving ministers; spinsters with nipped breasts and pursed mouths. I stood on the path, terrified for a moment at the starkness and universality of shrouds; at the infinite dead of the island, their heads pointing westward in a dense shoal, adrift on the slow tide that sets towards eternity.

My dreaming feet brought me to a low tombstone set in the east wall:

HERE LIES BURIED
A FOREIGN SEAMAN,
OF UNKNOWN NAME AND NATIONALITY,
WHOM THE SEA CAST UP ON THIS ISLAND,
JUNE THE SIXTH, 1856

*"Though I take the wings of
the morning, and flee to the
uttermost places of the sea."*

I closed my eyes and saw a little Basque town between the bay and the mountains.

The feast of Our Lady of the Sea was over. The nets and the oars had been blessed. The candles were still burning in their niches among the rocks.

Now the young people are dancing in a square that lies white and black under the moon.

The musician slouches, as if he were drunk or half asleep, against the fountain. Only his hand is alive, hovering over the string like a vibrant bird.

The young people are dancing now in long straight lines. The partners clap their hands and bow to each other. They shout; the dark faces are lit up with a flash of teeth. They move round each other with momentarily linked arms. They incline towards each other, their hands on their knees, and stamp their feet. It is all precision, disciplined fluency, a stylised masque of coupling.

Older men and women sit gossiping on the doorsteps. Occasionally they sip from tall glasses. One, a fat man with a yellow beard, looks often through a gap in the houses, at a ship anchored in the harbour.

An old shawled woman stands alone, in the shadow of the church. No one speaks to her; the seal of separation is on her. She is the guardian of the gates of birth and death. In this village she comes to deliver every wailing child, she goes to shroud every quiet corpse. Her eyes are in the dust, from which all this vanity has come, and to which it must return.

The hand over the guitar moves into a new swirling rhythm. Now the square is all one coloured wheel, a great wavering orange blossom.

Suddenly there is an interruption. A tall bearded sailor appears at an alley-opening and walks slowly across the square. The guitar falters. The dance is frozen. The old dark woman raises her head. The officer points to one of the dancers and crooks his finger: he must come, immediately, the ship is sailing tonight.

The seaman—he is only a boy—turns once and looks back. A girl has raised her apron to her face. The yellow-bearded man rises from his doorstep and makes a gesture of blessing: "Lady of Waters, guard him this day and all days till the sail returns to the headland."

Above the village a cross stands among the stars. Through a long silence comes the sound of the sea. The last votive candle gutters, and goes out among the rocks.

The little town of moonlight and music will never see that sail again. Her voyage has ended on a northern rock. All her sailors have vanished down the path of gull and lobster, scattered in a wild Atlantic storm. One broken shape only was lifted out of the seaweed. Curious hands have carried the nameless thing in procession across the fields. They have clipped the rags from it and combed its hair, and covered the crab-eaten face. And though there was no priest to sing Latin over it, a Calvinist minister said, "All flesh is grass, and the glory of flesh is as the flower thereof—the orange-blossom of Spain and the little blue Orkney primula, whose circles of beauty are full and radiant for a short time only; and then, drifting winterward, or broken with June tempest, lay separate shining arcs in the dust. . . ."

My slow circuitous walk had brought me to the new gaping hole in the earth. The grave-digger was still sitting on his barrow. He bored a sidelong glance into me and said: "There's only one way of coming into the world, but ah, God, there's two or three ways of going out."

"That's a fact," I said.

"Would you like," he said, "to see what a man *truly* is?"

Not understanding, I gave a quick nod. He groped with his hand into the small hill of clay beside the open grave, and brought out a skull. Carefully he wiped it on his moleskin trousers. "That's you," he said, "and me, and the laird, and Frank the idiot. Just that."

He laughed. "There's nothing here to make your face so white. It's as harmless as can be, this bone. It's at peace, and not before time. When it lived it had little rest, with its randy eyes and clattering tongue. This skull belonged to Billy Anderson, Moll's grandfather. He was twice in jail and fathered three illegitimate bairns. Oh, he was a thieving, drunken, fighting character, and it was a good day for him when we threw him in here. Wasn't it, Billy?" he said to the skull, blowing smoke into its eye-hollows. "Wasn't it, boy?" . . . The skull grinned back at him.

From the other side of the loch the school bell rang the dismissal.

Over the hill from the village, like a procession of beetles, came the mourners.

5

After I had finished my lessons that evening I was summoned into the shop.

My father was sitting at the counter between a barrel of paraffin oil and a great dark coil of tobacco. There was a jar of sweets at his elbow. Over his head hung jerseys and scarves and stockings, with price tickets on them. The lamp swung from the hook in the ceiling, smoking a little. There was always a good smell in the shop.

"It's thee, John," he said, raising his head from the ledger for a moment. "Sit down, boy." He counted the sticks of toffee in a glass jar and then said, "How did thu get on at the school today?"

"Fine," I said.

"I've been thinking about thee," he said, "what to make o' thee, once thee school-days are over."

He gathered up a handful of coins, and rang them one by one back into the till. Then he marked the ledger on his desk with a pencil.

"There's no future in this shop, I can tell thee that," he said. "The profits are getting smaller every year. The reason is, the folk are leaving the island. They're going to the cities and the colonies. Not a month passes but another family leaves.

"And then they send to the mail-order places in the south for their clothes and their ironmongery. A great lot of them do that. They forget that we depend on each other for our livelihood in a small island like this.

"And there's debts too," he said. "For instance, Mistress Anderson who was buried this afternoon died owing more than six pounds. So it'll be a poor inheritance for thee, this shop," he said.

He licked his pencil and wrote more figures in the ledger. His hair glittered frailly in the lamplight.

"I had a word with Miss Ingsetter this afternoon about thee," he went on. "She called at the shop after school for some fly-papers. She seemed surprised thu weren't home yet. . . . I made a point of asking her about thee. She says thu're an able boy, good beyond the general run at reading and writing and history. Not so bright at the mathematics. Sometimes thu're inclined to be inattentive and dreamy, she says. At times, only at times. But there's no harm in the boy, she said, and he's by no means stupid. And it's my opinion, she said, he ought to go to the grammar school in Kirkwall for a secondary education, once he turns twelve."

"I want to be a sailor," I said.

"The dreaminess," he said, "you take from your mother. . . . After the school comes the university. That'll cost money, a power of money. Still, I'm not barehanded, I haven't neglected to provide for things like that. With a degree in thee pocket, thu could enter *the professions*. Think of that."

"It's the sea I have a hankering for," I said. "Uncle Ben said he could get me into the Saint Line, any time I wanted."

"The ministry is an honourable profession," he said. "There isn't a lot of money in it, but you get a free manse, and I can tell you old MacFarland doesn't spend a fortune on food. He gets a hen here and a pound of butter there and a sack of tatties from the other place. On his rounds, you understand, his visitations. Cheese at the Bu, and fish from Quoys, and a fleece for spinning from Westburn, all for nothing. And nobody can say the work is strenuous."

"Supper is ready," my mother sang out from the kitchen.

"Now doctoring is strenuous, there's no doubt about that. They haven't a moment to call their own. They can't even be sure of a night's sleep. There's always somebody thundering at Dr Leslie's door after midnight with the toothache, or a pain in the guts, or a hook's got stuck in their hand. It's no wonder he's taken to the drink lately. But, putting all that aside, medicine is a fine calling. Plenty of money in it too, if you can get them to pay their bills."

"I spoke to Mother," I said. "She would like fine for me to be a deep-sea captain. She's going to write to Ben."

"The law," he said, "is a different thing. Not that there's anything wrong with it, if you understand, but there's a shady side to it, there's a certain amount of trickery about it that makes the ordinary honest man wonder sometimes. You can hardly open a newspaper without seeing some lawyer or other in trouble for embezzling his client's money, and carrying on. You'll hear a couple of them arguing a case like mad in the courts, and then, half an hour later, there they'll be walking down the street together cheek by jowl . . . John," he said, "never go to law if you can possibly help it. Not but what there aren't honest lawyers too."

He unscrewed the lid from a bottle of black-striped balls. He took out a couple between his fingers and handed them across the counter.

"If there's one place I have a longing to see," I said, "it's Japan."

He suddenly withdrew his hand and dropped the black-striped balls back into the jar.

"Not before your food," he said, licking his fingers. "I forgot. . . . Then there's teaching – "

"Are you coming for your supper," chanted my mother impatiently, "or are you not?"

Outside, the dog began to bark. There was a clattering of hoofs and wheels over the cobbles. The poultry squawked like mad in the yard. "Mercy," said my father, running to the door, "it's the tinkers. *The hens!*"

I followed him out, into the moonlight. The tinker's cart was opposite the door now. Abraham sat on the shaft. He cracked his whip and cried to the grey pony. In the cart sat Mary his wife with an infant slung behind her in a tartan shawl. Sarah walked alongside with her arms full of wild lupins.

They were going to the other end of the island where the rabbits were thick, to camp there.

"Giddap!" cried Abraham and cracked his whip. "That's a fine dog you have there, Mister Sigurdson," he shouted to my father. "I'll take a half-pound of bogey roll, and I'll pay you when I come back along next week."

"No," said my father sternly, "you'll pay now, for you owe me sixteen and six already."

"Hello, Sarah," I said. She stood on the road and looked at me through the dark blue congregated spires of lupins.

"Are you seeking a tin pail, mistress?" yelled Abraham to my mother who had come out and was standing at the corner of the house guarding the hens.

"Yes," she said, "I'll need one when you come back by next week."

Suddenly my father was furious. "We need no tin pails!" he shouted. "There's plenty of tin pails in the shop!"

"Next week-end, mistress," cried Abraham. He stood between the shafts and cracked his whip. "Giddap!" he yelled. The wheels rolled in crazy circles over the cobbles and stars streamed from the pony's hoofs. There was a sudden wild *cluck-cluck-clucking* from inside the cart as it moved off. Sarah stood looking at us, smiling through her screen of lupins.

My father went back into the shop, muttering. My mother stood at the corner of the house and watched them out of sight. "One of the hens is missing," she said. "I darena tell thee father. He would have the police at them for sure."

A wave of purple blossom rose in front of the moon and showered over me.

Soon the racket died away at the far end of the village. Sarah's mockery sounded from a distance of three fields. I turned back into the house. My face was wet with dew and petals, and the moon raged above the mission hall wilder than ever.

"The very idea!" cried my father from inside the shop. "A sailor! A tin pail! *The thieves!*"

Time was skulls and butterflies and guitars.

The Wedding

Iain Crichton Smith

IT WAS a fine blowy sunshiny day as I stood outside the church on the fringe of the small groups who were waiting for the bride to arrive. I didn't know anybody there; I was just a very distant relative, and I didn't feel very comfortable in my dark suit, the trousers of which were rather short. There were a lot of young girls from the Highlands (though the wedding was taking place in the city) all dressed in bright summery clothes and many of them wearing corsages of red flowers. Some wore white hats which cast intricate shadows on their faces. They all looked very much at ease in the city and perhaps most of them were working there, in hotels and offices. I heard one of them saying something about a Cortina and another one saying it had been a Ford. They all seemed to know each other and one of them said in her slow soft Highland voice, "Do you think Murdina will be wearing her beads today?" They all laughed. I wondered if some of them were university students.

The minister who was wearing dark clothes but no gown stood in the doorway chatting to the photographer who was carrying an old-fashioned black camera. They seemed to be savouring the sun as if neither of them was used to it. The doors had been open for some time as I well knew since I had turned up rather early. A number of sightseers were standing outside the railings taking photographs and admiring the young girls who looked fresh and gay in their creamy dresses.

I looked at the big clock which I could see beyond the church. The bride was late, though the groom had already arrived and was talking to his brother. He didn't look at all nervous. I had an idea that he was an electrician somewhere and his suit didn't seem to fit him very well. He was a small person with a happy rather uninteresting face, his black hair combed back sleekly and plastered with what was, I imagined, fairly cheap oil.

After a while the minister told us we could go in if we wanted to, and we entered. There were two young men, one in a lightish suit and another in a dark suit, waiting to direct us to our seats. We were asked which of the two we were related to, the bride or the groom, and seated accordingly, either on the left or the right of the aisle facing the minister. There seemed to be more of the groom's relatives than there were of the bride's and I wondered idly whether the whole thing was an exercise in psychological warfare, a primitive pre-marital battle. I sat in my seat and picked up a copy of a church magazine which I leafed through while I waited: it included an attack on Prince Philip for encouraging Sunday sport. In front of me a young girl who appeared to be a foreigner was talking to an older companion in broken English.

The groom and the best man stood beside each other at the front facing the minister. After a while the bride came in with her bridesmaids, all dressed in blue, and they took their positions to the left of the groom. The bride was wearing a long white dress and looked pale and nervous and almost somnambulant under the white head-dress. We all stood up and sang a psalm. Then the minister said that if there was anyone in the church who knew of any impediment to the marriage they should speak out now or forever hold their peace. No one said anything (one wondered if anyone ever stood up and accused either the bride or groom of some terrible crime): and he then spoke the marriage vows, asking the usual questions which were answered inaudibly. He told them to clasp each other by the right hand and murmured something about one flesh. The groom slipped the ring on to the bride's finger and there was silence in the church for a long time because the event seemed to last interminably. At last the ring was safely fixed and we sang another hymn and the minister read passages appropriate to the occasion, mostly from St Paul. When it was all over we went outside and watched the photographs being taken.

Now and again the bride's dress would sway in the breeze and a woman dressed in red would run forward to arrange it properly, or at least to her own satisfaction. The bride stood gazing at the camera with a fixed smile. A little boy in a grey suit was pushed forward to hand the bride a horseshoe, after which he ran back to his mother, looking as if he was about to cry. The bride and groom stood beside each other facing into the sun. One couldn't tell what they were thinking of or if they were thinking of anything. I suddenly thought that this must be the greatest day in the bride's life and that never again would a thing so public, so marvellous, so hallowed, happen to her. She smiled all the time but didn't speak. Perhaps she was lost in a pure joy of her own. Her mother took her side, and her father. Her mother was a calm, stout, smiling woman who looked at the ground most of the time. Her father twisted his neck about as if he were being chafed by his collar, and shifted his feet now and again. His strawy dry hair receded from his lined forehead and his large reddish hands stuck out of his white cuffs.

Eventually the whole affair was over and people piled into the taxis which would take them to the reception. I didn't know what to make of it all. It had not quite had that solemnity which I had expected and I felt that I was missing or had missed something important considering that a woman to the right of me in church had been dabbing her eyes with a small flowered handkerchief all through the ceremony. Both bride and groom seemed very ordinary and had not been transfigured in any way. It was like any other wedding one might see in the city, there didn't seem to be anything Highland about it at all. And the bits of conversation that I had overheard might have been spoken by city people. I heard no Gaelic.

For some reason I kept thinking of the father, perhaps because he had seemed to be the most uncomfortable of the lot. Everyone else looked so assured as if they had always been doing this or something like this and none of it came as a surprise to them. I got into a taxi with some people and without being spoken to arrived at the hotel which was a very good one, large and roomy, and charging, as I could see from a ticket at the desk, very high prices.

We picked up either a sherry or whisky as we went in the door and I stood about again. A girl in a white blouse was saying to her friend dressed in creamy jacket and suit, "It was in Luigi's you see and this chap said to me out of the blue, 'I like you but I don't know if I could afford you'." She giggled and repeated the story a few times. Her friend said: "You meet queer people in Italian restaurants. I was in an Indian restaurant last week with Colin. It doesn't shut till midnight you know. . . ." I moved away to where another group of girls was talking and one of them saying: "Did you hear the story about the aspirin?" They gathered closely together and when the story was finished there was much laughter.

After a while we sat down at the table and watched the wedding party coming in and sitting down. We ate our food and the girl on my left spoke to another girl on her left and to a boy sitting opposite her. She said: "This chap came into the hotel one night very angry. He had been walking down the street and there was this girl in a blue cap dishing out Barclaycards or something. Well, she never approached him at all though she picked out other people younger than him. He was furious about it, absolutely furious. Couldn't she see that he was a businessman, he kept saying. He was actually working in insurance and when we offered him a room with a shower he wouldn't take it because it was too expensive."

The other girl, younger and round-faced, said: "There was an old woman caught in the lift the other day. You should have heard the screaming. . . ." I turned away and watched the bride who was sitting at the table with a fixed smile on her face. Her father, twisting his neck about, was drinking whisky rapidly as if he was running out of time. Her mother smiled complacently but wasn't speaking to anyone. The minister sat at the head of the table eating his chicken with grave deliberation.

"Did you hear that Lindy has a girl?" said the boy in front of me to the girls.

"And she's thinking of going back home."

They all laughed. "I wouldn't go back home now. They'll be at the peats," said the girl on my left.

"Well," said the boy, "I don't know about that. There was a student from America up there and he wanted to work at the peats to see what it was like. He's learned to speak Gaelic too."

"How did he like it?" said the girl at my left.

"He enjoyed it," said the boy. "He said he'd never enjoyed anything so much. He said they'd nothing like that in America."

"I'm sure," said the small girl and they laughed again.

"Wouldn't go back for anything anyway," said the girl to my left. "They're all so square up there."

When we had all finished eating, the Master of Ceremonies said that the groom would make a speech which he did very rapidly and incoherently. He was followed by the best man who also spoke very briefly and with incomprehensible references to one of the bridesmaids who blushed deeply as he spoke. There were cheers whenever an opportunity arose such as, for instance, when the groom referred for the first time to his wife and when there was a reference to someone called Tommy.

After that the telegrams were read out. Most of them were quite short and almost formal, "Congratulations and much happiness" and so on. A number, however, were rather bawdy, such as, for instance, one which mentioned a chimney and a fire and another which suggested that both the bride and groom should watch the honey on their honeymoon. While the telegrams were being read some of the audience whispered to each other, "That will be Lachy", and "That will be Mary Anne". I thought of those telegrams coming from the Highlands to this hotel where waitresses went round the tables with drinks and there were modernistic pictures, swirls of blue and red paint, on the walls. One or two of the telegrams were in Gaelic and in some strange way they made the wedding both more authentic and false. I didn't know what the bride thought as she sat there, as if entranced and distant. Everything seemed so formal, so fixed and monotonous, as if the participants were trying to avoid errors, which the sharp-witted city-bred waitresses might pick up.

Eventually the telegrams had all been read and the father got up to speak about the bride. I didn't know what I expected but he certainly began with and air of business-like trepidation. "Ladies and gentlemen," he said, "I am here today to make a speech, which as you will know is not my speciality." He twisted his neck about inside the imprisoning collar and continued. "I can tell you that the crossing was good and the skipper told me that the *Corona* is a good boat though a bit top-heavy." He beamed nervously and then said, "But to my daughter. I can tell you that she has been a good daughter to me. I am not going to say that she is good at the peats, for she is never at home for the peats and she never went to the fishing as girls of her age used to do in the past." By this time people were beginning to look at each other or down at their plates and even the waitresses were smiling. "I'll tell you something about the old days. We turned out good men and women in those days, good sailors who fought for their country. Nowadays I don't know about that. I was never in the city myself and I never wore a collar except to the church. Anyway I was too busy. There were the calves to be looked after and the land as you all know. But I can tell you that my daughter here has never been a burden to us. She has always been working on the mainland. Ever since she was a child she has been a good girl with no nonsense and a help to her mother, and many's the time I've seen her working at the hay and in the byre. But things is changed now. Nowadays, it's the tractors and not the horses. In the old days too we had the gig, but now it's the train and the plane." The bride was turning a deadly white and staring down at the table. The girls on my left were transfixed. Someone dropped a fork or a spoon or a knife and the sound it made could be heard quite clearly. But the father continued remorselessly: "In my own place I would have spoken in the Gaelic, but even the Gaelic is dying out now as anyone can read in the papers every week. In the old days too we would have a wedding which would last for three days. When Johnny Murdo married, I can remember it very well, the wedding went on for four days. And he married when he was quite old. But as for my daughter here, I am very happy that she is getting married, though the city is not the place for me and I can tell you I'll be very glad to get back to the dear old home again. And that is all I have to say. Good luck to them both."

When he sat down there was a murmur of conversation which rose in volume as if to drown the memory of the speech. The girls beside me talked in a more hectic way than ever about their hotels and made disparaging remarks about the islands and how they would never go back. Everyone avoided the bride who sat fixed and miserable at the table as if her wedding dress had been turned into a shroud.

I don't know exactly what I felt. It might have been shame that the waitresses had been laughing. Or it might have been gladness that someone had spoken naturally and authentically about his own life. I remember I picked up my whisky and laid it down again without drinking it and felt that this was in some way a meaningful action.

Shortly afterwards the dancing began in an adjoining room. During the course of it (at the beginning they played the latest pop tunes) I went over and stood beside the father who was standing by himself in a corner looking miserable as the couples expressed themselves (rather than danced) in tune to the music, twisting their bodies, thrusting out their bellies and swaying hypnotically with their eyes half shut.

"It's not like the eightsome reel," I said.

"I don't know what it is like," he said. "I have never seen anything like it."

"It is rather noisy," I agreed. "And how are the crops this year?" I said to him in Gaelic.

He took his dazed eyes off a couple who were snapping their fingers at each other just in front of him, and said: "Well, it's been very dry so far and we don't know what we're going to do." He had to shout the words against the music and the general noise. "I have a good few acres, you know, though a good many years ago I didn't have any and I worked for another man. I have four cows and I sell the milk. To tell you the honest truth I didn't want to come here at all but I felt I couldn't let her down. It wasn't an easy thing for me. I haven't left the island before. Do you think this is a posh hotel?"

I said that I thought it was. He said. "I tell you I've never been in a hotel before now. They've got a lot of carpets, haven't they? And mirrors, I've never seen so many mirrors."

"Come on," I shouted, "let's go into the bar." We did so and I ordered two beers.

"The people in there aren't like human beings at all," he said. "They're like Africans."

After a while he said, "It was the truth I said about her, she's never at home. She's always been working in hotels. I'll tell you something, she's never carried a creel on her back, though that's not a good thing either. She was always eating buns and she would never eat any porridge. What do you think of her husband, eh? He was talking away about cars. And he's got a good suit, I'll give him that. He gave the waiter a pound, I saw it with my own eyes. Oh, he knows his way around hotels, I'll be bound. But where does he come from? I don't know. He's never ploughed any ground, I think."

I thought at that moment that he wouldn't see his daughter very often in the future. Perhaps he really was without knowing it, giving her away to a stranger in a hired cut-price suit.

After a while we thought it politic to go back. By this time there was a lull in the dancing and the boy in the lightish suit had started a Gaelic song, but he didn't know all the words of it, only the chorus. People looked round for assistance while red-faced and embarrassed he kept asking if anyone knew the words because he himself had lost them. Suddenly the father pushed forward with authority and standing with his glass in his hand began to sing—verse after verse in the traditional manner. They all gathered round him and even the waitresses listened, there was so much depth and intensity in his singing. After he had finished there was much applause and requests for other songs, for he seemed to know the words of all of them. The young girls and the boys gathered round him and sat on the floor in a circle looking up at him. He blossomed in the company and I thought that I could now leave, for he seemed to be wholly at home and more so than his audience were.

Glossary

ahint   behind
aik   oak
ain   own
auld   old

bairn   a child
banes   bones
begude   began
behove   to be obliged
beil   to fester
bestial   livestock
bide   to wait; to remain where you are
bieldy   snug
billy   a young fellow; a lover; a comrade
birk   a birch tree
birn   a burden
bissim   a rogue (*bissom*—a lewd and worthless woman)
bogle   an apparition; a ghost
bonnie   beautiful; fine; pretty
braeface   hillside
braw (brae)   fine
breeks   trousers
breid   bread
brunstane   brimstone
brunt   burned
bure   bore
burn   a stream

callant   a stripling; a lad
caller   fresh

caller ben healthily indoors
canny careful; cautious
cantrip magic spell; trick; piece of mischief
cam' came
carline an old wife; a hag
cauld cold
chaft the jaw-bone
chalmer room; upper room
change-house alehouse
chap knock; strike
clachan a village which has a church
claught to lay hold of forcibly and suddenly
claverin' chattering
clour a blow
coats petticoats
collie-shangie an uproar
corbie a carrion crow
corp a corpse
cottar house a farm labourer's house
craig the neck; the throat
cried called
cuist to cast; to throw off
cummer a contemptuous term for a woman

daffin' playing idly; sporting about
dawtie darling; pet
dead gemmie an exclamation of delight
deave to stun with noise
deidly deadly
deil a devil; the Devil
deil a' never a . . .
denner dinner
dirl to rattle; to vibrate noisily
dominie a schoolmaster
door cheeks doorposts
dowg a dog
dreepin' dripping
duds shabby clothes
dunt thump
dwalled dwelt
dwine to dwindle; to waste away
dyke a wall of stone or turf

e'en eyes
eldritch unearthly; ghastly

fa' fall

fash   to trouble
feck   an abundance
feint the much   little
fell   really (an intensive): thus, *fell on*—precisely on
fitba'   football
fleyed   scared
flyte   to rage at
focht   fought
forbye   besides; moreover
forjaskit   jaded
forrit   forward: *to come forrit*—to offer oneself as a communicant
frae   from
fremyt   strange; far off
frichtit   frightened
fuff   spit; hissing sound
fushionless   feeble

gaads   finery
gab   talk; conversation
gable end   the end wall of a building
gaed   went
gane   gone
gang   to go: *gang your ain gate*—to go your own way
gangrel   a vagrant
gart   caused
girn or grin   a grimace; a snarl
glisk   a glimpse; to glimpse
gloamin'   twilight
glower   a threatening look
goun   gown
gousty   stormy; tempestuous
gowk   a fool; a blockhead
greet   to weep
grogram   heavy corded silk
grooze   to shudder
grue   to shudder
grund   ground; land
guid   good
guidman   master of the house; a husband
, *guttery*   muddy

habber   to stammer; to make inarticulate noises
hae   to have
hail   whole
hap   to cover for warmth
hasp   a latch

haud   to hold
het   hot
hinder   rear
hirstle   to breathe roughly and noisily
hoots   an exclamation of doubt, contempt or irritation
howff   a shelter; a retreat; a den

ilka   each

jaloose   to guess; to suspect

keek   to peep
ken   to know
kye   cattle

laigh   low
laird   landlord
lane   alone: *your lane*—alone
lave   the rest, the others
leddy   lady
leed   lead
leevin'   living
letten a be   let be
ley   grassland
licht   light
limmer   a rascal; a loose woman; a playful term applied to a woman rather
   contemptuously
linkin'   moving at speed
loon   a boy; a lad; a ragamuffin
lowed   glowed
lown   still
lowsed   freed; lost
loup   to jump; to throb; to swell with anger
lug   ear

mair   more
mane   to moan
manse   a Scottish minister's official dwelling
mear   mare
meat   food; victuals
meck   a halfpenny; a ha'penny
meddle   to interfere
meikle   great
micht nae   might not
midden   a rubbish dump
minister   a Presbyterian clergyman
mirk   dark; murky

mistryst   to vex without cause
mony   many: *mony's the time*—often and often
moo   mouth
muckle   large; great
muir   moor
mutch   a woman's cap

neb   a nose
neist   next
nellie   a term of abuse
neuk   a corner; fold in a garment
nicht   night
nieve   fist
nip   a small glass of whisky
noo   now

orra man   a farm labourer who does small jobs
out o' the gate   out of the way
ower   over; too
owercome   the refrain or chorus of a song
oxter   armpit

paichin'   gasping; puffing
pechin'   gasping; puffing
pibroch   Highland bagpipe music
pickle   a few
pit-mirk   pitch-dark
plaid   a cloak; a blanket
pleiter   a mess
powney   a pony
press   a wall cupboard with shelves
prigg   to ask; to plead
pu'   to pull
puir   poor

queans   girls

rairin'   roaring
redd   to set in order
reishlin'   rustling noisily
rig-end   ridge-end
roust   to rouse
rummle   to rumble; to stir violently

sabbin'   making a hissing noise
sae   so
sair   sore
sark.   a chemise; a night-dress

saugh   the sighing of the wind
saughs   willows
sauls   souls
scruff   the back of the neck
scunner   a feeling of loathing
seelent   silent
seepin'   oozing
sharn   cow dung
shaw   a flat piece of ground at the foot of a hill or steep bank
shawed   showed
sholtie   a pony
shoon   shoes
shot   one's turn in a game
shouther   shoulder
sib   closely related
sic   such
siccan   suchlike
sinsyne   since then
skelloch   a shriek; a yell
skelp   to smack; to wallop with gusto
skeugh   squint; distorted
skirl   to screech
skrieghan   shrieking
slocken   to slake
smeddum   mettle; force of character
smoor   to smother; to drown
sodger   soldier
soss   muddle
spate   flood
spunkies   will-o'-the-wisps; fire creatures
stammy-gastered   astonished
steeked   shut tight
steer   to stir; to bustle
stook   a bundle of corn-sheaves
stramp   to tread; to stomp
stravage   to wander about
strynge   strange
suld   should
sumph   a soft, rather stupid, person
suspeckit   suspected
swack   supple; active
swat   sweat
sweir   lazy
syne   then; ago

108

tackety hobnailed
tap top
tashed wearied out
tauld told
thir these
thirled bound to; dependent on
thrapple windpipe
thrawn twisted; perverse; stubborn
threep to harp on about
thretty thirty
tink a tinker
tottie very small
toun town
trauchle a drudge
treviss a stall in a stable
trig neat and tidy
twal' twelve
tyke a coarse dog

uncanny weird; dangerous
unco strange
unhaly unholy
unstreakit not laid out for burial
upsittin' forward; ambitious; superior in one's own estimation

wa' wall
wad would
wae's me woe is me
wan one
want to be without
wat wet
weans children
weary wearisome; disastrous
weel well
whammle to tumble about
whaten what
wheep a shrill cry or whistle
whiles times; at times
whill which
wise in one's right mind
wud mad
wydit waded

yett gate
yowlin' howling and barking